THE VANISHING ACT OF ESME LENNOX

Also by Maggie O'Farrell

After You'd Gone
My Lover's Lover
The Distance Between Us

THE VANISHING ACT
OF ESME LENNOX

Maggie O'Farrell

headline
review

First published in Great Britain in 2006
by Headline Review
An imprint of Headline Book Publishing

1

Cataloguing in Publication Data is available from the British Library.

Hardback 0 7553 0843 3 (ISBN-10)
Hardback 978 0 7553 0843 9 (ISBN-13)
Trade paperback 0 7553 3222 9 (ISBN-10)
Trade paperback 978 0 7553 3222 9 (ISBN-13)

Typeset in Weiss by
Palimpsest Book Production Limited, Polmont, Stirlingshire

Endpapers: from a fabric design in the collection of the
Victoria & Albert Museum, London/© V & A Images.

Printed and bound in Great Britain by Clays Ltd, St Ives plc

Headline's policy is to use papers that are natural, renewable and recyclable
products and made from wood grown in sustainable forests. The logging
and manufacturing processes are expected to conform to the
environmental regulations of the country of origin.

HEADLINE BOOK PUBLISHING
A division of Hodder Headline
338 Euston Road
London NW1 3BH

www.reviewbooks.co.uk
www.hodderheadline.com

for Saul Seamus

Much Madness is divinest Sense –
To a discerning eye –
Much Sense – the starkest Madness –
'Tis the Majority
In this, as All, prevail –
Assent – and you are sane –
Demur – and you're straightaway dangerous –
And handled with a Chain –

                                        Emily Dickinson

I couldn't have my happiness made out of a wrong –
an unfairness – to somebody else . . . What sort of a
life could we build on such foundations?

                                        Edith Wharton

L et us begin with two girls at a dance.

They are at the edge of the room. One sits on a chair, opening and shutting a dance-card with gloved fingers. The other stands beside her, watching the dance unfold: the circling couples, the clasped hands, the drumming shoes, the whirling skirts, the bounce of the floor. It is the last hour of the year and the windows behind them are blank with night. The seated girl is dressed in something pale, Esme forgets what, the other in a dark red frock that doesn't suit her. She has lost her gloves. It begins here.

Or perhaps not. Perhaps it begins earlier, before the party, before they dressed in their new finery, before the candles were lit, before the sand was sprinkled on the boards, before the year whose end they are celebrating began. Who knows? Either way it ends at a grille covering a window with each square exactly two thumbnails wide.

If Esme cares to gaze into the distance – that is to say, at what lies beyond the metal grille – she finds that, after a while, something happens to the focusing mechanism of her eyes. The squares of the grille will blur and, if she concentrates long enough, vanish. There is always a moment before her body reasserts itself, readjusting her eyes to the proper reality of the world, when it is just her and the trees, the road, the beyond. Nothing in between.

The squares at the bottom are worn free of paint and you can see the different layers of colour inside each other, like rings in a tree. Esme is taller than most so can reach the part where the paint is new and thick as tar.

Behind her, a woman makes tea for her dead husband. Is he dead? Or just run off? Esme doesn't recall. Another woman is searching for water to pour on flowers that perished long ago in a seaside town not far from here. It is always the meaningless tasks that endure: the washing, the cooking, the clearing, the cleaning. Never anything majestic or significant, just the tiny rituals that hold together the seams of human life. The girl obsessed with cigarettes has had two warnings already and everyone is thinking she is about to get a third. And Esme is thinking, where does it begin — is it there, is it here, at the dance, in India, before?

She speaks to no one, these days. She wants to concentrate, she doesn't like to muddy things with the distraction of speech. There is a zoetrope inside her head and she doesn't like to be caught out when it stops.

Whir, whir. Stop.

In India, then. The garden. Herself aged about four, standing on the back step.

Above her, mimosa trees are shaking their heads at her, powdering the lawn with yellow dust. If she walked across it, she'd leave a trail behind. She wants something. She wants something but she doesn't know what. It's like an itch she can't reach to scratch. A drink? Her *ayah*? A sliver of mango? She rubs at an insect bite on her arm and pokes at the yellow dust with her bare toe. In the distance somewhere she can hear her sister's skipping-rope hitting the ground and the short shuffle of feet in between. Slap shunt slap shunt slap shunt.

She turns her head, listening for other noises. The brrr-cloop-brrr of a bird in the mimosa branches, a hoe in the garden soil – scritch, scritch – and, somewhere, her mother's voice. She can't make out the words but she knows it's her mother talking.

Esme jumps off the step, so that both feet land together, and runs round the side of the bungalow. Beside the lily pond, her mother is bending over the garden table, pouring tea into a cup, her father beside her in a hammock. The edges of their white clothes shimmer in the heat. Esme narrows her eyes until her parents blur into two hazy shapes, her mother a triangle and her father a line.

She counts as she walks over the lawn, giving a short hop every tenth step.

'Oh.' Her mother looks up. 'Aren't you having your nap?'

'I woke up.' Esme balances on one leg, like the birds that come to the pond at night.

'Where's your *ayah*? Where's Jamila?'

'I don't know. May I have some tea?'

Her mother hesitates, unfolding a napkin across her knee. 'Darling, I rather think—'

'Give her some, if she wants it.' Her father says this without opening his eyes.

Her mother pours tea into a saucer and holds it out. Esme ducks under her outstretched hand and clambers on to her lap. She feels the scratch of lace, the heat of a body underneath white cotton. 'You were a triangle and Father was a line.'

Her mother shifts in the seat. 'I beg your pardon?'

'I said, you were a triangle—'

'Mmm.' Her mother's hands grip Esme's arms. 'It's really too hot for cuddles today.' Esme is set down on the grass again. 'Why not go and find Kitty? See what she's up to.'

'She's skipping.'

'Couldn't you join in?'

'No.' Esme reaches out and touches the frosted icing on a bun. 'She's too—'

'Esme,' her mother lifts her wrist clear of the table, 'a lady waits to be offered.'

'I just wanted to see what it felt like.'

'Well, please don't.' Her mother leans back in the chair and shuts her eyes.

Esme watches her for a moment. Is she asleep? A blue vein pulses in her neck and her eyes move under the lids. Tiny globes of water, no bigger than pinheads, are pushing out from the skin above her lip. Where her shoe straps end and skin begins, her mother's feet bloom red marks. Her stomach is distended, pushed out with another baby. Esme has felt it, wriggling like a caught fish. Jamila says she thinks this one is lucky, that this one will live.

Esme looks up at the sky, at the flies circling the lily flowers on the pond, at the way her father's clothes protrude from the underside of the hammock in diamonds of loose cloth. In the distance, she can still hear Kitty's skipping-rope, the scritch, scritch of the hoe – or is it a different one? Then she hears the drone of an insect. She turns her head to see it but it's gone, behind her, to the left of her. She turns again but it's closer, the buzz louder, and she feels the catch of its feet in her hair.

Esme springs up, shaking and shaking her head but the buzzing is louder still and suddenly she feels the crawling flutter of wings on her ear. She shrieks, flailing at her head with her hands but the buzzing is deafening now, blocking out all other sounds, and she feels the insect edging inside the narrow passage of her ear – and what will happen, will it eat through her eardrum and into her brain and will she be deaf like the girl in Kitty's book? Or will she die? Or will it live in her head and she will have this noise inside her for ever?

She lets out another piercing shriek, still shaking her hair, staggering about the lawn, and the shriek turns to sobs and just as the buzzing starts to lift and the insect backs out of her ear, she hears her father saying, 'What is the matter with the child?' and her mother calling across the lawn for Jamila.

Could this be her earliest memory? It might be. A beginning of sorts – the only one she remembers.

Or it might be the time Jamila painted a lacework of henna across her palm. She saw her lifeline, her heartline interrupted by a new pattern. Or Kitty falling into the pond and having to be fished out and taken into the house in a towel. Playing jacks with the cook's children outside the garden's perimeter. Watching the earth around the muscular trunk of the banyan tree boiling with ants. It could just as easily have been these.

Perhaps it was this. A lunch when she was strapped to a chair, the binding tight across her middle. Because, as her mother announced to the room, Esme must learn to behave. Which, Esme knew, meant not getting out of her chair until the meal was finished. She loved the space under the table, you see, they couldn't keep her from it, the illicit privacy under the cloth. There is something peculiarly touching about people's feet. Their shoes, worn down in odd places, the idiosyncrasies in lace-tying, blisters, calluses, who crossed their ankles, who crossed their knees, whose stockings had holes, who wore mismatched socks, who sat with a hand in whose lap – she knew it all. She would slip from her chair, lithe as a cat, and they couldn't reach to hook her out.

The binding is a scarf that belongs to her mother. It has a pattern Esme likes: repeating swirls in purple, red and blue. Paisley, her mother says it is called, which Esme knows is a place in Scotland.

The room is full. Kitty is there, her mother, her father and some guests – several couples, a girl with scandalously short hair, whom her mother has placed opposite a young engineer, an elderly woman and her son, and a lone man, seated next to Esme's father. Esme thinks, but she's not entirely sure, that they are all eating soup. She seems to recall the lift and dip of spoons, the clash of metal on china, the discreet suck and swallow.

They are talking, on and on. What can there be to say? So many things, it seems. Esme can never think of anything, not one thing, she would wish to impart to these people. She is pushing her spoon to one side of the bowl, then back, seeing how the soup swirls and eddies around the silver. She is not listening, or at least not to the words, but tuning her hearing to the collective noise of them. It is like that of parrots in high trees, or a gathering of frogs at dusk. The same grrp-grrp-grrp sound.

Suddenly and without warning, they all get up. They put down their spoons, leap from their chairs and rush from the room. Esme, daydreaming, thinking about soup eddies, about frogs, has missed something. Everyone is talking excitedly as they go and Kitty jostles against their father to get out of the door first. Their mother, in her eagerness, has forgotten about Esme, tethered to her chair.

She watches, spoon in hand, mouth open. The doorway swallows them, the engineer guest last, and she hears their feet disappear down the passageway. She turns back in astonishment to the empty room. Lilies stand, proud and impassive, in a glass vase; the clock counts down seconds, a napkin slips to a chair. She thinks about yelling, about opening her lungs and shouting. But she doesn't. She looks at the curtains, trembling at the open window, a fly settling on a plate. She holds out her arm and uncurls her fingers, just to see what will happen. The spoon drops in a straight line, bounces once off its curved end, does a somersault in the air, then slides along the carpet and comes to rest under the sideboard.

Iris walks along the street, keys in one hand, coffee in the other. The dog is just behind her, claws tick-ticking on the concrete. Ladders of sun drop down through the gaps in the high buildings and the night's rain is vanishing in patches from the pavement.

She crosses the road, the dog following close behind. She aims a kick at a beer can left on the doorstep but instead of rolling across the pavement, as she'd hoped it would, it tips sideways, spraying beer over the shop entrance.

'Damn you,' Iris says. 'Damn you, damn you.'

She kicks it again in fury and, empty now, it clatters into the gutter. Then she casts a glance over her shoulder. Impassive stone tenements rear up, glittering with rows of unblinking windows. She looks down at the dog. He waves his tail and gives a faint whine.

'It's all right for you,' she says.

She yanks at the shutter over the door, so that it retracts

back into its roller with a shocked rattle. She steps over the puddle of beer on the threshold, pulling a pile of letters from the sprung trap of the letterbox. She shuffles through them as she crosses the shop. Bills, bills, bank statement, postcard, bills, and a brown envelope, sealed down in a V.

The typeface on the front makes her pause, half-way to the counter. It is small, cramped, each letter heavy with ink, the semi-circular heart of the *e* obliterated. Iris holds the envelope close to her face and sees that the shapes have been pressed into the grain of the manila paper. She is running her fingertips over them, feeling the indentations, realising that it has been done on a typewriter.

A draught of cold air snakes in, curling about her ankles. She lifts her head and looks around the shop. The blank, featureless heads of the hatstands stare down at her, a silk coat hung from the ceiling sways slightly in the breeze. She lifts the flap and the seal gives easily. She unfolds the single white sheet, glances down it. Her mind is still running on the beer, on how she's going to clean it up, how she must learn not to kick cans in the street, but she catches the words *case* and *meeting* and the name *Euphemia Lennox*. At the bottom, an illegible signature.

She is about to start again at the beginning when she remembers that she has some detergent in the tiny kitchen at the back of the shop. She crams the letter and the rest of the post into a drawer and disappears through a heavy velvet curtain.

She emerges on to the pavement with a mop and a bucket of soapy water. She starts with the outside of the door, sluicing water towards the street. She turns her face up to the sky. A van passes on the road, close enough so that her hair is lifted by the backdraught. Somewhere out of sight a child is crying. The dog stands in the doorway, watching the tiny figures of people walking along the bridge high above them. Sometimes this street feels so deep cut into the city it's as if Iris is leading a subterranean existence. She leans on the mop handle and surveys her doorstep. The name *Euphemia Lennox* resurfaces in her mind. She thinks, it's probably an order of some sort. She thinks, lucky I kept that bucket. She thinks, it looks like rain.

Iris sits opposite Alex in a bar in the New Town. She swings a silver shoe off the end of one toe and bites down on an olive. Alex toys with the bracelet on her wrist, rolling it between his fingers. Then he glances at his watch. 'She's never usually this late,' he murmurs. His eyes are hidden behind dark glasses that give Iris back a warped reflection of herself, of the room behind her.

She drops the olive stone, sucked clean, into a dish. She'd forgotten that Alex's wife, Fran, was joining them. 'Isn't she?' Iris reaches for another olive, presses it between her teeth.

Alex says nothing, shakes a cigarette out of its box, lifts it to his mouth. She licks her fingers, swirls her cocktail around her glass. 'You know what?' she says, as he searches for a match. 'I got an invoice today and next to my name it had "the witch" scribbled on it. In pencil.'

'Really?'

'Yeah. "The witch". Can you believe that? I can't remember who it was now.'

He is silent, striking a match against its box, raising the flame to his mouth. He takes a long draw on his cigarette before saying, 'Obviously it was someone who knows you.'

Iris considers her brother for a moment as he sits before her, smoke curling from his mouth. Then she reaches out and drops an olive down the front of his shirt.

Fran hurries into the bar. She's late. She's been at the hairdresser's. She has her medium-brown hair streaked blonde every six weeks. It hurts. They yank sections of her hair through a tight cap, and daub it with stinging chemicals. She has a headache so bad that she feels as if she's still wearing the cap.

She scans the bar. She's put on her silk blouse, the one Alex likes. He once said it made her breasts look like peaches. And her narrow linen skirt. Her clothes rustle and her new hair hangs in a clean curtain around her face.

She sees them, half hidden by a column. They are bent together, close together, under the lights. They are drinking the same drink – something clear and red, clinking with ice – and their heads are almost touching. Iris is in a pair of trousers that sits low on her hips. She's still skinny, the jut of her hipbones rising above the waistband. She's wearing a top that seems to have had its collar and cuffs scissored off.

'Hi!' Fran waves but they don't see her. They are holding hands. Or maybe not. Alex's hand rests on Iris's wrist.

Fran makes her way through the tables, clutching her bag to her side. When she reaches them, they are exploding into laughter and Alex is shaking his shirt, as if something is caught in it.

'What's so funny?' Fran says, standing between them, smiling. 'What's the joke?'

'Nothing,' Alex says, still laughing.

'Oh, go on,' she cries, 'please.'

'It's nothing. Tell you later. Do you want a drink?'

Across the city, Esme stands at a window. To her left, a flight of stairs stretches up; to her right, the stairs sink down. Her breath masses on the cool glass. Needles of rain are hitting the other side and dusk is starting to colour in the gaps between the trees. She is watching the road, the two lines of traffic unwinding in contrary motion, the lake behind, ducks drawing lines on the slate surface.

Down on the ground, cars have been leaving and arriving all day. People climb in, through one of the back doors, the engine is fired and the cars leave, gobbling gravel as they swing round the bend. Bye, the people at the door call, waving their hands in the air, byebyebye.

'Hey!' The shout comes from above her.

Esme turns. A man is standing at the top of the stairs. Does she know him? He looks familiar but she's not sure.

'What are you doing?' the man cries, surprisingly exasperated for someone Esme thinks she's never met. She doesn't know how to answer, so doesn't.

'Don't dawdle at the window like that. Come on.'

Esme takes one last look at the driveway and sees a woman who used to have the bed next to her, standing beside a brown car. An old man is stowing a suitcase in the boot. The woman is weeping and peeling off her gloves. The man doesn't look at her. Esme turns and starts climbing the stairs.

Iris climbs into the window display of her shop. She eases the velvet suit off the mannequin, shaking it out, pairing up the seams of the trousers, placing it on a hanger. Then she goes to the counter and unwraps, from layers and layers of muslin protectors, a folded dress in scarlet. She takes it up carefully by the shoulders, gives it a shake and it opens before her like a flower.

She walks towards the light of the window with it spread over her hands. It's the kind of piece she gets only rarely. Once in a lifetime, almost. *Haute couture*, pure silk, a famous design house. When a woman had called and said she had been clearing out her mother's cupboards and had found some 'pretty frocks' in a trunk, Iris hadn't expected much. But she'd gone along anyway. The woman had opened the trunk and, among the usual crushed hats and faded skirts, Iris had seen a flash of red, a bias-cut hem, a tapered cuff.

Iris eases it over the mannequin's shoulders, then works round it, tugging at the hem, straightening an armhole, adding a pin or two at the back. The dog watches from his basket with amber eyes.

When she's finished, she goes out on to the pavement and studies her efforts. The dog follows her to the doorway and stands there, panting lightly, wondering if a walk is in the offing. The dress is flawless, tailored perfection. Half a century old and there isn't a mark on it – perhaps it was never worn. When Iris asked the woman where her mother might have got it, she had shrugged and said, she went on a lot of cruises.

'What do you think?' Iris asks the dog, taking a step back, and he yawns, showing the arched pink rafters of his mouth.

Inside, she turns the mannequin forty-five degrees so it looks as if the figure in the red dress is about to step out of the window and on to the street. She searches in the room at the back of the shop for a boxy, sharp-cornered handbag and lays it at the mannequin's feet. She goes outside to have another look. Something isn't quite right. Is it the angle of the mannequin? The snakeskin shoes?

Iris sighs and turns her back on the window. She is edgy about this dress and she isn't sure why. It's too perfect, too good. She isn't used to dealing with things that are so untouched. Really, she knows, she would like to keep it.

But she stamps on the thought immediately. She cannot keep it. She hasn't even allowed herself to try it on because if she did she'd want never to take it off. You cannot afford to keep it, she tells herself severely. Whoever buys it will love it. At that price, they'd have to. It will go to a good home.

For want of something to do, she pulls out her mobile and dials Alex's. She casts another, baleful, look at the window as she hears the ringtone click off and she inhales, ready to speak. But Fran's voice is on the line: 'Hi, Alex's phone.' Iris pulls her mobile away from her ear and shuts it with a snap.

In the middle of the afternoon, a man comes in. He spends a long time wiping his shoes on the mat, darting glances around the room. Iris smiles at him, then bends her head back over her book. She doesn't like to be too pushy. But she watches from under her fringe. The man strikes out across the empty middle of the shop and, arriving at a rack of négligés and camisoles, rears away like a frightened horse.

Iris puts down her book. 'Can I help you with anything?' she says.

The man reaches for the counter and seems to hold on to it. 'I'm looking for something for my wife,' he says. His face is anxious and Iris sees that he loves his wife, that he wants to please her. 'Her friend told me she likes this shop.'

Iris shows him a cashmere cardigan in the colour of heather, she shows him a pair of Chinese slippers embroidered with orange fish, a suede purse with a gold clasp, a belt of crackling alligator skin, an Abyssinian scarf woven in silver, a corsage of wax flowers, a jacket with an ostrich-feather collar, a ring with a beetle set in resin.

'Do you want to get that?' the man says, lifting his head.

'What?' Iris asks, hearing at the same time the ring of the phone under the counter. She ducks down and snatches it up. 'Hello?'

Silence.

'Hello?' she says, louder, pressing her hand over her other ear.

'Good afternoon,' a cultured male voice says. 'Is this a convenient time to talk?'

Iris is instantly suspicious. 'Maybe.'

'I'm calling about –' the voice is obliterated by a blast of static on the line, reappearing again a few seconds later '– and meet with us.'

'Sorry, I missed that.'

'I'm calling about Euphemia Lennox.' The man sounds slightly aggrieved now.

Iris frowns. The name rings a distant bell. 'I'm sorry,' she says, 'I don't know who that is.'

'Euphemia Lennox,' he repeats.

Iris shakes her head, baffled. 'I'm afraid I don't—'

'Lennox,' the man repeats, 'Euphemia Lennox. You don't know her?'

'No.'

'Then I must have the wrong number. My apologies.'

'Wait a sec,' Iris says but the line cuts out.

She stares at the phone for a moment, then replaces the receiver.

'Wrong number,' she says to the man. His hand, she sees, is hovering between the Chinese slippers and a beaded clutchbag with a tortoiseshell fastening. He lays it on the bag.

'This,' he says.

Iris wraps it for him in gold tissue paper.

'Do you think she'll like it?' he asks, as she hands him the parcel.

Iris wonders what his wife is like, what kind of a person she might be, how strange it must be to be married, to be tightly bound, clipped like that to another. 'I think she will,' she replies. 'But if she doesn't, she can bring it back and choose something else.'

After she has shut the shop for the night, Iris drives north, leaving the Old Town behind, through the valley that once held a loch, traversing the cross streets of the New Town and on, towards the docks. She parks the car haphazardly in a residents-only bay and presses the buzzer on the outer door of a large legal firm. She's never been here before. The building seems deserted, an alarm light blinking above the door, all windows dark. But she knows Luke is in there. She leans her head towards the intercom, expecting to hear the relay of his voice. There's nothing. She presses it again and waits. Then she hears the door unlocking from the other side and it swings out towards her.

'Ms Lockhart,' he says. 'I take it you have an appointment?'

Iris looks him up and down. He is in a shirt, the tie loose at the neck, the sleeves rolled back. 'Do I need one?'

'No.' He reaches out, seizes her wrist, then her arm, then her shoulder, and pulls her over the threshold towards him. He kisses her neck, pulling the door shut with one hand, while the other is working its way inside her coat, up and under the hem of her blouse, round her waist, over her breast, up the dents in her spine. He half carries, half drags her up the stairs and she stumbles in her heels. Luke catches her elbow and they burst in through a glass door.

'So,' Iris says, as she rips apart his tie and flings it aside, 'does this place have security cameras?'

He shakes his head as he kisses her. He is struggling with the zip of her skirt, swearing with effort. Iris covers his hands with her own and the zip gives, the skirt slides down and she kicks it off her feet, high into the air, making Luke laugh.

Iris and Luke came across each other two months ago at a wedding. Iris hates weddings. She hates them with a passion. All that parading about in ridiculous clothes, the ritualised publicising of a private relationship, the endless speeches given by men on behalf of women. But she quite enjoyed this one. One of her best friends was marrying a man Iris liked, for a change; the bride had a beautiful outfit, for a change; there had been no seating plans, no speeches and no being herded about for horrible photographs.

It was Iris's outfit that had done it – a backless green crêpe-de-Chine cocktail dress she'd had specially altered.

She had been talking to a friend for some time but had still been aware of the man who had sidled up next to them. He was looking about the marquee with an air of calm assurance as he sipped his champagne, as he waved at someone, as he passed a hand through his hair. When the friend said, 'That's quite a dress, Iris,' the man had said, without looking at them, without even leaning towards them, 'But it isn't really a dress. Isn't it what used to be called a gown?' And Iris looked at him properly for the first time.

He had proved to be a good lover, as Iris had known he would. Considerate without being too conscientious, passionate without being clingy. Tonight, however, Iris is beginning to wonder if she is sensing the slightest hint of haste in his movements. She opens her eyes and regards him through narrowed lids. His eyes are closed, his face rapt, concentrated. He lifts her, hoisting her from the desk to the floor and, yes, Iris sees him – she definitely sees him – cast a look at the clock above the computer.

'My God,' he says afterwards, too soon afterwards, Iris feels, before their breathing has returned to normal, before their hearts have slowed in their chests, 'can you drop in every evening?'

Iris rolls on to her stomach, feeling the prickly nap of the carpet against her skin. Luke kisses the small of her back, running his hand up and down her spine for a moment. Then he hoists himself upright, walks to the desk, and Iris watches as he gets dressed. There is an urgency to the way he does it, yanking up his trousers, jerking on his shirt.

'Expected at home?' Iris, still lying on the floor, makes sure to enunciate every word.

He glances at his watch as he straps it to his wrist and grimaces. 'I told her I'd be working late.'

She reaches for a paperclip that has fallen to the carpet and, as she starts to untwist it, remembers irrelevantly that they are called *trombones* in French.

'I should call her, actually,' Luke mutters. He sits on his desk and reaches for the phone. He drums his fingers as he waits, then smiles at Iris – a wide, quick grin that disappears when he says, 'Gina? It's me. No. Not yet.'

Iris tosses aside the paperclip, elongated out of shape, and reaches for her knickers. She doesn't have a problem with Luke's wife but she doesn't particularly want to have to listen to his conversations with her. She gathers her clothes off the floor, one by one, and dresses. She is sitting to zip up her boots when Luke hangs up. The floor judders as he comes towards her. 'You're not going?' he says.

'I am.'

'Don't.' He kneels, wrapping his arms round her waist. 'Not yet. I told Gina I wouldn't be home for a while. We could get a carry-out. Are you hungry?'

She straightens his collar. 'I've got to go.'

'Iris, I want to leave her.'

Iris freezes. She makes to get out of the chair but he is holding her fast. 'Luke—'

'I want to leave her and be with you.'

For a moment, she is speechless. Then she starts to prise his fingers off her waist. 'For God's sake, Luke. Let's not have this conversation. I have to go.'

'You do not. You can stay for a bit. We need to talk. I can't do this any more. It's driving me mad, pretending everything's fine with Gina when every minute of the day I'm desperate to—'

'Luke,' she says, brushing one of her hairs from his shirt, 'I'm going. I said I might go to the cinema with Alex and—'

Luke frowns and releases her. 'You're seeing Alex tonight?'

Luke and Alex have met once and only once. Iris had been seeing Luke for a week or so when Alex turned up unannounced at her flat. He has a habit of doing this whenever Iris has a new man. She could swear he has a sixth sense for it.

'This is Alex,' she had said, as she walked back into the kitchen, her jaw tight with irritation, 'my brother. Alex, this is Luke.'

'Hi.' Alex had leant over the kitchen table and offered his hand.

Luke had stood and taken her brother's hand. His broad-knuckled fingers covered all of Alex's. Iris was struck by their physical contrast: Luke a dark, hulking mesomorph next to Alex's lanky, fair-skinned ectomorph. 'Alexander,' he said, with a nod, 'it's good to meet you.'

'Alex,' Alex corrected.

'Alexander.'

Iris looked up at Luke. Was he doing that deliberately? She felt dwarfed suddenly, diminished by both of them towering above her. 'It's Alex,' she snapped. 'Now sit down, will you, both of you, and let's have a drink.'

Luke sat. Iris got an extra glass for Alex and slopped in some wine. Luke was looking from her to Alex and back again. He smiled.

'What?' Iris said, putting the bottle down.

'You don't look at all alike.'

'Well, why would we?' Alex cut in. 'No blood relation, after all.'

Luke seemed confused. 'But I thought—'

'She's my step.' Alex glanced at Luke. 'Step-sister,' he clarified. 'My father married her mother.'

'Oh.' Luke inclined his head. 'I see.'

'She didn't say?' Alex asked, reaching for the bottle of wine.

When Luke went to the bathroom, Alex leant back in his chair, lit a cigarette, glanced round the kitchen, brushed ash from the table, adjusted his collar. Iris eyed him. How dare he sit there, contemplating the light fittings? She picked up her napkin, folded it into a long strip and thwacked it hard across his sleeve.

He brushed more ash from his shirt front. 'That hurt,' he remarked.

'Good.'

'So.' Alex drew on his cigarette.

'So what?'

'Nice top,' he said, still looking away from her.

'Mine or his?' Iris retorted.

'Yours.' He turned his head towards her. 'Of course.'

'Thanks.'

'He's too tall,' Alex said.

'Too tall?' she repeated. 'What do you mean?'

Alex shrugged. 'I don't know if I could ever get on with someone that much bigger than me.'

'Don't be ridiculous.'

Alex ground his cigarette into the ashtray. 'Am I allowed to ask what the . . .' he circles his hand in the air '. . . situation is?'

'No,' she said quickly, then bit her lip. 'There is no situation.'

Alex raised his eyebrows. Iris twisted her napkin into a rope.

'Fine,' he murmured. 'Don't tell me, then.' He jerked his head towards the door, towards the sound of footsteps on bare boards. 'Lover boy's coming back.'

Esme sits at the schoolroom table, slumped to one side, her head resting on her forearm. Across the table, Kitty is doing French verbs in an exercise book. Esme isn't looking at the arithmetic that has been set for her. She looks instead at the dust swarming in the light beams, the white line of Kitty's parting, the way the knots and markings in the wood of the table flow like water, the oleander branches outside in the garden, the faint crescent moons that are appearing from under her cuticles.

Kitty's pen scratches on the page and she sighs, frowning in concentration. Esme thuds her heel against the chair leg. Kitty doesn't look up. Esme does it again, harder, and Kitty's chin lifts. Their eyes meet. Kitty's lips part in a smile and her tongue pokes out, just enough for Esme to see but not enough for their governess, Miss Evans, to notice. Esme grins. She crosses her eyes and sucks in her cheeks, and Kitty has to bite her lip and look away.

But with her back to the room, facing out to the garden, Miss Evans intones, 'I am hoping that the arithmetical exercise is nearing completion.'

Esme looks down at the strings of numbers, plus signs, minus signs. At the side of the two lines that mean equals there is nothing: a black void. Esme has a flash of inspiration. She moves her slate to one side and slides off her chair. 'May I be excused?' she says.

'May I be excused . . . ?'

'May I be excused, please, Miss Evans?'

'For what reason?'

'A . . .' Esme struggles to remember what she's meant to say. 'A . . . um . . .'

'A call of nature,' Kitty says, without looking up from her verbs.

'Was I addressing you, Kathleen?'

'No, Miss Evans.'

'Then kindly hold your tongue.'

Esme breathes in through her nose, and as she lets it out very slowly through her mouth, she says, 'A call of nature, Miss Evans.'

Miss Evans, still with her back to them, inclines her head. 'You may. Be back here within five minutes.'

Esme skips along the courtyard, brushing her hand against the blossoms that grow in pots along the wall. Petals cascade in her wake. The heat of the day is reaching its peak. Soon it will be time for a sleep, Miss Evans will disappear until tomorrow, and she and Kitty will be allowed to lie inside the haze of their mosquito nets, watching the slow circles of the ceiling fan.

At the dining-room door, she stops. Where now? From the dank interior of the kitchen comes the hot, buttery smell of *chai*. From the veranda, she can hear the murmur of her mother's voice: '. . . he would insist on taking the lake road even though I'd made it perfectly clear we were to go straight to the club, but as you know . . .'

Esme turns and wanders up the other side of the courtyard towards the nursery. She pushes at the door, which feels dry and sun-hot under her palm. Inside, Jamila is stirring something on a low stove and Hugo is standing, holding on to a chair leg, a wooden block pressed to his mouth. When he sees Esme, he lets out a shriek, drops to the floor and starts crawling towards her with a jerky, clockwork motion.

'Hello, baby, hello, Hugo,' Esme croons. She loves

Hugo. She loves his dense, pearly limbs, the dents over his knuckles, the milky smell off him. She kneels down to him and Hugo seizes her fingers, then reaches up for one of her plaits. 'Can I pick him up, Jamila?' Esme begs. 'Please?'

'It is better not to. He is very heavy. Too heavy for you, I think.'

Esme presses her face to Hugo's, nose to nose, and he laughs, delighted, his fingers gripping her hair. Jamila's sari shushes and whispers as she comes across the room and Esme feels a hand on her shoulder, cool and soft.

'What are you doing here?' Jamila murmurs, stroking her brow. 'Isn't it time for lessons?'

Esme shrugs. 'I wanted to see how my brother was.'

'Your brother is very well.' Jamila reaches down and lifts Hugo on to her hip. 'He misses you, though. Do you know what he did today?'

'No. What?'

'I was on the other side of the room and he—'

Jamila breaks off. Her wide black eyes fix on Esme's. In the distance they can hear Miss Evans's clipped voice and Kitty's, speaking over it, anxious and intervening. Then the words become clear. Miss Evans is telling Esme's mother that Esme has slipped away again, that the girl is impossible, disobedient, unteachable, a liar . . .

And Esme finds that, in fact, she is sitting at a long table in the canteen, a fork held in one hand, a knife in the other. In front of her is a plate of stew. Circles of grease float on the surface, and if she tries to break them apart, they just splinter and breed into multiple, smaller clones of themselves. Bits of carrot and some type of meat lump up under the gravy.

She won't eat it. She won't. She'll eat the bread but not with the margarine. That she'll scrape off. And she'll drink the water that tastes of the metal cup. She won't eat the orange jelly. It comes in a paper dish and is smirred with a film of dust.

'Who's coming for you?'

Esme turns. There is a woman next to her, leaning towards her. The wide scarf tied round her forehead has slipped, giving her a vaguely piratical air. She has drooping eyelids and a row of rotting teeth. 'I beg your pardon?' Esme says.

'My daughter's coming,' the pirate woman says, and clutches her arm. 'She's driving here. In her car. Who's coming for you?'

Esme looks down at her tray of food. The stew. The grease circles. The bread. She has to think. Quick. She has to say something. 'My parents,' she hazards.

One of the kitchen women squeezing tea out of the urn laughs and Esme thinks of the cawing of crows in high trees.

'Don't be stupid,' the woman says, pushing her face up to Esme's. 'Your parents are dead.'

Esme thinks for a moment. 'I knew that,' she says.

'Yeah, right,' the woman mutters, as she bangs down a teacup.

'I did.' Esme is indignant, but the woman is moving off down the aisle.

Esme shuts her eyes. She concentrates. She tries to find her way back. She tries to make herself vanish, make the canteen recede. She pictures herself lying on her sister's bed. She can see it. The mahogany end, the lace counterpane, the mosquito net. But something is not right.

She was upside-down. That was it. She swivels the image in her head. She had been lying on her back, not her front, her head tipped over the end, looking at the room upside-down. Kitty was walking in and out of her vision, from the wardrobe to the trunk, picking up and dropping items of clothing. Esme was holding a finger against one nostril, breathing in, then held the finger against the other, breathing out. The gardener had told her it was the way to serenity.

'Do you think you'll have a nice time?' Esme asked.

Kitty held a chemise up to the window. 'I don't know. Probably. I wish you were coming.'

Esme took her finger away from her nose and rolled on to her stomach. 'Me too.' She kicked a toe against the bedhead. 'I don't see why I have to stay here.'

Her parents and sister were going 'up country', to a house party. Hugo was staying behind because he was too little and Esme was staying behind because she was in disgrace for having walked along the driveway in bare feet. It had happened two days ago, on an afternoon so scorching her feet wouldn't fit into her shoes. It hadn't even occurred to her that it wasn't allowed until her mother rapped on the drawing-room window and beckoned her back inside. The pebbles of the driveway had been sharp under her soles, pleasurably uncomfortable.

Kitty turned to look at her for a moment. 'Perhaps Mother will relent.'

Esme gave the bedhead a final, hefty kick. 'Not likely.' A thought struck her. 'You might stay here. You might say you don't feel well, that—'

Kitty started pulling the ribbon out of the chemise. 'I should go.'

Her tone – taut, affected resignation – pricked Esme's curiosity. 'Why?' she said. 'Why should you go?'

Kitty shrugged. 'I need to meet people.'

'People?'

'Boys.'

Esme struggled to sit up. 'Boys?'

Kitty wound the ribbon round and round her fingers. 'That's what I said.'

'What do you want to meet boys for?'

Kitty smiled down at her ribbon. 'You and I,' she said, 'will have to find someone to marry.'

Esme was thunderstruck. 'Will we?'

'Of course. We can't very well spend the rest of our lives here.'

Esme stared at her sister. Sometimes it felt that they were equals, the same age, but at others the six years between them stretched out, an impossible gap. 'I'm not going to get married,' she announced, hurling herself back to the bed.

Across the room, Kitty laughed. 'Is that right?' she said.

Iris is late. She overslept, she took too long over breakfast and in deciding what to wear. And now she is late. She is due to interview a woman about helping in the shop on Saturdays and she is going to have to take the dog with her. She is hoping the woman won't mind.

She has her coat over her arm, her bag on her shoulder, the dog on his lead and is just about to leave when the phone rings. She hesitates for a moment, then slams the door and runs back to the kitchen, which excites the dog, who thinks she's playing a game and he leaps up at her, tangling Iris in the lead so that she trips and falls against the kitchen door.

She curses, rubbing her shoulder, and lunges for the phone. 'Yes, hello,' she says, holding the phone and the dog lead in one hand, her coat and bag in the other.

'Am I speaking with Miss Lockhart?'

'Yes.'

'My name is Peter Lasdun. I am calling from—'

Iris doesn't catch the name but she hears the word 'hospital'. She clutches at the receiver, her mind leap-frogging. She thinks: my brother, my mother, Luke. 'Is someone . . . Has something happened?'

'No, no,' the man chuckles irritatingly, 'there's no cause

for alarm, Miss Lockhart. It's taken us some time to track you down. I am contacting you about Euphemia Lennox.'

A mixture of relief and anger surges through Iris. 'Look,' she snaps, 'I have no idea who you people are or what you want but I've never heard of Euphemia Lennox. I'm really very busy and—'

'You're her contact family member.' The man states this very quietly.

'What?' Iris is so annoyed that she drops bag, coat and dog lead. 'What are you talking about?'

'You are related to Mrs Kathleen Elizabeth Lockhart, née Lennox, formerly of Lauder Road, Edinburgh?'

'Yes.' Iris looks down at the dog. 'She's my grandmother.'

'And you have had enduring power of attorney since . . .' there is the scuffling of papers '. . . since she went into full-time nursing care.' More paper scuffling. 'I have here a copy of a document lodged with us by her solicitor, signed by Mrs Lockhart, naming you as the family member to be contacted about affairs pertaining to one Euphemia Esme Lennox. Her sister.'

Iris is really cross now. 'She doesn't have a sister.'

There is a pause in which Iris can hear the man moving his lips over his teeth. 'I'm afraid I must contradict you,' he says eventually.

'She doesn't. I know she doesn't. She's an only one, like me. Are you telling me I don't know my own family tree?'

'The trustees of Cauldstone have been trying to trace—'

'Cauldstone? Isn't that the – the . . .' Iris fights to come up with a word other than *loony-bin* '. . . asylum?'

The man coughs. 'It's a unit specialising in psychiatry. Was, I should say.'

'Was?'

'It's closing down. Which is why we are contacting you.'

As she is driving down Cowgate, her mobile rings. She wrests it from her coat pocket. 'Hello?'

'Iris,' Alex says, into her ear, 'did you know that two and a half thousand left-handed people are killed every year using things made for right-handed people?'

'I did not know that, no.'

'Well, it's true. It says so here, right in front of me. I'm working on a home-safety website today, such is my life. I thought I should ring and warn you. I had no idea that your existence was so precarious.'

Iris glances at her left hand, gripping the steering-wheel. 'Neither did I.'

'The worst culprits are tin-openers, apparently. Though it doesn't say exactly how you can die from using one. Where've you been all morning? I've been trying to get hold of you for hours with this piece of news. I thought you'd emigrated without telling me.'

'Unfortunately I'm still here.' She sees a traffic-light ahead turn amber, presses the accelerator and the car leaps beneath her. 'It's been an average day, so far. I had breakfast, I interviewed someone for the shop and I found out that I'm responsible for a mad old woman I never knew existed.'

Behind him, in his office, she hears the shug-shug-shug of a printer. 'What?' he says.

'A great-aunt. She's in Cauldstone.'

'Cauldstone? The loony-bin?'

'I got a call this morning from—' Without warning, a van swings out in front of her and she slams her fist on the horn and shouts, 'Bastard!'

'Are you driving?' Alex demands.

'No.'

'Have you got Tourette's, then? You are driving. I can hear you.'

'Oh, stop fussing,' she starts to laugh, 'it's fine.'

'You know I hate that. I'm always convinced I'll have to listen to you dying in a car crash. I'm hanging up. Goodbye.'

'Wait, Alex—'

'I'm going. Stop taking calls while you're driving. I'll speak to you later. Where are you going to be?'

'At Cauldstone.'

'You're going there today?' he asks, suddenly serious.

'I'm going there now.'

She hears Alex tapping a pen on his desk, him shifting about in his seat. 'Don't sign anything,' he says eventually.

*

'But I don't understand,' Iris interrupts. 'If she is my grandmother's sister, my . . . my great-aunt, then why have I
never heard of her?'

Peter Lasdun sighs. The social worker sighs. The two of
them exchange a look. They have been sitting in this room,
round this table, for what feels like hours. Peter Lasdun has
been painstakingly outlining for Iris what he refers to as
Routine Policies. These include Care Plans, Community Care
Assessments, Rehabilitation Programmes, Release Schedules.
He seems to talk permanently in capital letters. Iris has managed
to offend the social worker – or Key Worker, as Lasdun calls
her – by mistaking her for a nurse, causing her to start reeling
off her social-work qualifications and university degrees. Iris
would like a glass of water, she would like to open a window,
she would like to be somewhere else. Anywhere else.

Peter Lasdun takes a long time lining up a file with the
lip of his desk. 'You haven't discussed Euphemia with any
members of your family,' he asks, with infinite patience,
'since our conversation?'

'There's no one left. My grandmother is away in the world
of Alzheimer's. My mother's in Australia and she's never
heard of her. It's possible that my father would have known,
but he's dead.' Iris fiddles with her empty coffee cup. 'It all
seems so unlikely. Why should I believe you?'

'It's not unusual for patients of ours to . . . shall we say,
fall out of sight. Euphemia has been with us a long time.'

'How long exactly?'

Lasdun consults his file, running a finger down the pages.

The social worker coughs and leans forward. 'Sixty years, I believe, Peter, give or take—'

'Sixty years?' Iris almost shouts. 'In this place? What's wrong with her?'

This time, they both take refuge in their notes. Iris leans forward. She's quite adept at reading upside-down. *Personality disorder*, she manages to decipher, *bi-polar, electro-convulsive* — Lasdun sees her looking and snaps the file shut.

'Euphemia has had a variety of diagnoses from a variety of . . . of professionals during her stay at Cauldstone. Suffice to say, Miss Lockhart, my colleague and I have worked closely with Euphemia during our recent schedule of Rehabilitation Programmes. We are fully convinced of her docility and are very confident about her successful rehabilitation into society.' He treats her to what he must think is a caring smile.

'And I suppose,' Iris says, 'that this opinion of yours has nothing to do with the fact that this place is being closed down and sold for its land value?'

He fidgets with a pot of pens, taking two out, laying them on the desk, then putting them back. 'That, of course, is another matter. Our question to you is,' he gives her that wolfish smile again, 'are you willing to take her?'

Iris frowns. 'Take her where?'

'Take her,' he repeats. 'House her.'

'You mean . . .' she is appalled '. . . with me?'

He gestures vaguely. 'Anywhere you see fit to—'

'I can't,' she says. 'I can't. I've never met her. I don't know her. I can't.'

He nods again, wearily. 'I see.'

On the other side of the table, the social worker is shuffling her piles of paper together. Peter Lasdun brushes something off the cover of his file.

'Well, I thank you for your time, Miss Lockhart.' Lasdun ducks down behind the desk, reaching for something on the floor. Iris sees, as he resurfaces, that it is another file, with another name. 'If we need your input on any matters in the future, we will be in touch. Someone will show you out.' He gestures towards the reception desk.

Iris sits forward in her chair. 'Is that it? End of story?'

Lasdun spreads his hands. 'There is nothing further to discuss. It is my job, as representative of the hospital, to put this question to you, and you have duly answered.'

Iris stands, fiddling with the zip on her bag. She turns and takes two steps towards the door. Then she stops. 'Can I see her?'

The social worker frowns. Lasdun looks at her blankly. 'Who?'

His mind is already on the next file, Iris sees, the next reluctant set of relatives. 'Euphemia.'

He pinches the skin between his eyes, twists his wrist to glance at his watch. He and the social worker look at each other for a moment. Then the social worker shrugs.

'I suppose,' Lasdun says, with a sigh. 'I'll get someone to take you down.'

*

Esme is thinking about the hard thing. The difficult one. She does this only rarely. But sometimes she gets the urge and today is one of those days when she seems to see Hugo. In the corner of her eye, a small shape crawling through the shadow in the lee of a door, the space beneath the bed. Or she can hear the pitch of his voice in a chair scraped across the floor. There's no knowing how he might choose to be with her.

There are women playing snap at the table across the room, and in the flack-flick of the cards is the noise of the ceiling fan that hung in the nursery. Oiled, stained wood it was. Utterly ineffective, of course. Just stirred the heavy air like a spoon in hot tea. It had been above her, churning the heat in the room. And she had been twirling a paper bird above his cot.

'Look, Hugo.' She made it fly down towards him then up, coming to rest on the bars. But he didn't put out his hand to try to seize it. Esme jiggled it again, near his face. 'Hugo. Can you see the bird?'

Hugo's eyes followed it but then he gave a sob, turning away, pushing his thumb into his mouth.

'He's sleepy,' said Jamila, from across the room where she was hanging nappies out to dry, 'and he has a slight fever. It may be his teeth. Why don't you go out into the garden for a while?'

Esme ran past the pond where the hammock swung empty, past the fleece of orange flowers round the banyan tree. She ran over the croquet lawn, dodging the hoops, down the path, through the bushes. She vaulted the fence and then she stopped. She shut her eyes, held her breath, and listened.

There it was. The weeping, the slow weeping, of rubber trees leaking their fluid. It sounded like the crackle of leaves a mile away, like the creeping of minute creatures. She had sworn to Kitty that she could hear it, but Kitty had raised her eyebrows. Esme tilted her head this way and that, still with her eyes shut tight, and listened to the sound of trees crying.

She opened her eyes. She looked at the sunlight splintering and re-forming on the ground. She looked at the spiral gashes in the trunks around her. She ran back, over the fence, over the croquet lawn, round the pond, filled with the glee of her parents being away, of having the run of the house.

In the parlour, Esme wound the gramophone, stroked the velvet curtains, rearranged the chain of ivory elephants on the windowsill. She opened her mother's workbox and examined the threads of coloured silk. She rolled back the carpet and spent a long time sliding in her stockinged feet. She discovered that she could slide all the way from the claw-footed chest to the drinks cabinet. She unlocked the glass bookcase and took down the leather-bound volumes, sniffed them, felt their gold-edged pages. She opened the piano and performed glorious glissandos up and down the keys. In her parents' bedroom, she sifted through her mother's jewellery, eased the lid off a box of powder and dabbed some on her cheeks. Her features, when she looked up into the oval mirror, were still freckled, her hair still wild. Esme turned away.

She climbed on to the polished end of her parents' bed, held out her arms and allowed herself to drop. The mattress came up to meet her – bouf! – her clothes billowing out, her hair flying. When the bed had stopped shaking, she lay there for a while, a disarray of skirts, pinafore, hair. She bit at a fingernail, frowning. She had felt something.

Esme straightened up, climbed back on to the bed-end, raised her arms, closed her eyes, fell to the mattress and – there. There it was again. A soreness, a tenderness in two points on her chest, a strange, exquisite kind of pain. She rolled on to her back and looked down. Under the white of her pinafore, everything was as it always had been. Esme raised a hand and pressed it against her chest. The pain spread outwards, like ripples on a pond. It made her sit up, meet her own eyes in the mirror again and she saw her face, flushed and shocked.

She wandered along the veranda, kicking at the dust that collected there every day. She would ask Kitty about it. The nursery, when she walked in, was dim and cold. Why weren't the lamps lit? There was a movement in the gloom, a rustle or a sigh. Esme could make out the muted white of the cot, the humped back of the settee. She stumbled forward into the dark, coming upon the daybed sooner than she'd expected. 'Jamila,' she said, and touched her arm. The *ayah*'s skin was sticky with sweat. 'Jamila,' Esme said again.

Jamila gave a slight jerk, sighed, and muttered something that contained 'Esme', and the name sounded as it always did when Jamila said it: Izme, Is Me.

'What was that?' Esme leant closer.

Jamila muttered again, a string of sounds in her own language. And there was something in those unfamiliar syllables that frightened Esme. She stood up. 'I'm going to get Pran,' she said. 'I'll be back in a minute.'

Esme ran out of the door and down the veranda. 'Pran!' she called. 'Pran! Jamila's ill and—' On the threshold of the kitchen, she stopped. Something was smouldering and cracking in the low stove and an oblong of light filtered in through the back door.

'Hello?' she said, one hand on the wall.

She stepped into the room. There were pots on the floor, a heap of flour in a basin, a knife buried in a sheaf of coriander. A fish lay filleted and ready on its side. Dinner was being prepared but it was as if they had all stepped outside for a minute, or vanished into the dirt floor, like drops of *ghee*.

She turned and walked back across the courtyard and, as she walked, it dawned on her that there were no voices. No sounds of servants calling to each other, no footfalls, no opening and slamming of doors. Nothing. Just the creaking of branches and a shutter banging somewhere on its hinges. The house, she realised, was empty. They had all gone.

Esme hurtled down the driveway, her lungs burning.

Darkness had fallen quickly and the branches overhead were black and restless in the sky. The gates were padlocked and beyond them she could see dense undergrowth, punctured by tiny lights moving in the dark.

'Excuse me,' she shouted. 'Excuse me, please.'

A group of men were standing in the distance, beside the road, the flare of a lamp illuminating their faces.

'Can you hear me?' she shouted, and rattled the gates. 'I need help. My *ayah* is ill and—'

They were moving off, muttering to each other, glancing back at her, and Esme was sure, she was absolutely certain, that one was the gardener's boy who used to give her rides on his shoulders.

In the nursery, she fumbled with matches and the lamp. The glow spread from where she was standing across the floor, up to the ceiling, along the walls, picking out the pictures of the gospels, the nursing chair, the bed where Jamila lay, the stove, the table where they ate, the shelf of books.

When there was enough light, she walked to the cot and the movement seemed to hurt her legs, as if she'd been sitting for a long time. At the edge of the cot, she discovered she was still holding the matches. She had to put them down before she could pick Hugo up and there was nowhere to put them so she had to bend and place them on the floor. And when she tried to pick him up it was difficult. She had to lean over and there were so many wraps and blankets and his body seemed much heavier and he was so cold and so stiff that it was hard to get a grip on him. He was frozen into the shape in which he always slept: on his back, arms stretched out, as if seeking an embrace, as if falling through space.

Later, Esme will tell people that she sat with him in the nursery all night. But they won't believe her. 'That's impossible,' they will say. 'You must have slept. You don't remember.' But she did. In the morning, as the light began to slide between the shutters, the matches were still on the floor next to her shoe, and the nappies were still drying beside the fire. She was never sure at what point Jamila died.

They found her in the library. She had locked herself in.

She remembers long hours of silence. A silence more absolute and powerful than anything she had ever imagined. The light fading and resurging. Birds passing through the trees like needles through fabric. Hugo's skin acquiring a delicate, pewter tinge. She thinks she just switched off, slowed down, an unwound clock. And then suddenly her mother was there, howling and screeching, and her father's face was pushed up close, shouting, where is everyone, where did they go. She'd been there for days, they said, but it felt longer to her, decades, or longer, infinitely long, several ice ages.

She wouldn't let them take Hugo. They had to prise him from her. It took her father and a man they'd got from somewhere. Her mother stood by the window until it was all over.

Iris, a nurse and the social worker descend in a lift. It seems to take a long time. Iris imagines they must be sinking into the bedrock that shores up the city. She steals a look at the social worker but her eyes are fixed on the illuminating floor numbers. In the nurse's pocket there is a small, boxed electronic device. Iris is wondering what it's for when she feels the lift do a gentle bounce and come to a stop. The doors open. There is a ribcage of bars before them. The nurse reaches out to tap in a code, but turns to Iris. 'Stay close,' she says. 'Don't stare.'

Then they are outside the bars, on the other side of the bars, the bars sliding shut behind them, in a corridor with striplighting and red-brown linoleum. There is the prickling stink of bleach.

The nurse sets off, the rubber grips on her shoe-soles squealing. They go through a set of swing doors, past rows and rows of locked rooms, a yellow-lit nurses' station, a pair of chairs screwed to the floor. On the ceiling, cameras blink and swivel to watch them go.

It takes Iris a while to work out what's odd about this place. She doesn't know what she expected – gibbering Bedlamites? howling madmen? – but it wasn't this ruminative quiet. Every other hospital she's ever been in has been crowded, teeming, corridors full of people, walking, queuing, waiting. But Cauldstone is deserted, a ghost hospital. The green paint on the walls gleams like radium, the floors are polished to a mirror. She wants to ask, where is everyone, but the nurse is entering a code into another door and suddenly a new smell hits her.

It's fetid, oppressive. Bodies left too long in the same

clothes. Food reheated too many times. Rooms where the windows are never thrown wide. They pass the first open door and Iris sees a mattress propped on its side, a couch covered with paper. She looks away and sees, outside the reinforced glass of the corridor, an enclosed garden. Paper, plastic cups and other litter swirl about the concrete. As she turns back, she catches the eye of the social worker. Iris is the first to look away. They pass through another set of doors and the nurse stops.

They enter a room with chairs lining the walls. Three women sit at a table playing cards. Weak sunlight trickles through narrow, high windows and a television mutters from the ceiling. Iris stands beneath it as the nurse confers with another nurse. A woman in a long, stretched grey cardigan comes up and stands before her, close, too close, shifting from foot to foot. 'Got a cigarette?' she says.

Iris steals a glance at her. She is young, younger than her maybe, her hair black at the roots but straw-yellow at the ends. 'No,' Iris says, 'sorry.'

'A cigarette,' she repeats urgently, 'please.'

'I haven't got any. I'm sorry.'

The woman doesn't respond and doesn't move away. Iris can feel the sour breath on her neck. Across the room, an elderly woman in a crumpled dress walks from one chair to the next, saying, in a clear, high voice, 'He's always tired when he comes in, always tired, very tired, so I'll need to put the kettle on.' Someone else sits in a ball, fists clenched over her head.

Then Iris hears the shout: 'Euphemia.'

A nurse waits in a doorway, hands on hips. Iris follows her gaze to the far end of the room. A tall woman stands on tiptoe at the high window, her back to them.

'Euphemia!' the nurse calls again, and rolls her eyes at Iris. 'I know she can hear me. Euphemia, you've got a visitor.'

Iris sees the woman turn, first her head, then her neck, then her body. It seems to take an extraordinarily long time and Iris is reminded of an animal uncurling from sleep. Euphemia lifts her eyes to Iris and regards her, the length of the room between them. She looks at the nurse, then back to Iris. She has one hand laced into the grille over the window. Her lips part but no sound comes out and, for a moment, it seems that she will not speak, after all. Then she clears her throat.

'Who are you?' Euphemia says.

'Charming!' the nurse interrupts loudly, so loudly that Iris wonders if Euphemia might be a little deaf. 'She doesn't get many visitors, do you, Euphemia?'

Iris starts walking towards her. 'I'm Iris,' she says. Behind her, she can hear the cigarette girl hiss Iris, Iris, to herself. 'You don't know me. I'm . . . I'm your sister's granddaughter.'

Euphemia frowns. They examine each other. Iris had, she realises, been expecting someone frail or infirm, a tiny geriatric, a witch from a fairytale. But this woman is tall, with an angular face and searching eyes. She has an air of slight hauteur, the expression arch, the brows raised. Although she must be in her seventies, there is something incongruously childlike about her. Her hair is held to one side with a clip and the dress she wears is flowered, with a full skirt – not an old woman's dress.

'Kathleen Lockhart is my grandmother,' Iris says, when she reaches her. 'Your sister. Kathleen Lennox?'

The hand at the window gives a small jerk. 'Kitty?'

'Yes. I suppose—'

'You are Kitty's granddaughter?'

'That's right.'

Without warning, Euphemia's hand shoots out and seizes her wrist. Iris cannot help herself: she jumps back, turning to look for the nurse, the social worker. Immediately Euphemia lets go. 'Don't worry,' she says, with an odd smile. 'I don't bite. Sit down, Kitty's granddaughter.' She lowers herself into a chair and points to the one next to her. 'I didn't mean to frighten you.'

'I wasn't frightened.'

She smiles again. 'Yes, you were.'

'Euphemia, I—'

'Esme,' she corrects.

'Sorry?'

She closes her eyes. 'My name,' she says, 'is Esme.'

Iris glances towards the nurses. Has there been a mistake?

'If you look at them once more,' Euphemia says, in a steady voice, 'just once more, they will come over and take me away. I shall be locked in solitary for a day, perhaps more. I would like to avoid this for reasons that I'm certain must be obvious to you, and I repeat to you that I won't hurt you and I promise that I mean it, so please don't look at them again.'

Iris swivels her gaze to the floor, to the woman's hands smoothing her dress over her knees, to her own feet laced into her shoes. 'OK. I'm sorry.'

'I have always been Esme,' she continues, in the same tone. 'Unfortunately, they only have my official name, the name on my records and notes, which is Euphemia. Euphemia Esme. But I was always Esme. My sister,' she gives Iris a sideways glance, 'used to say that "Euphemia" sounded like someone sneezing.'

'You haven't told them?' Iris asks. 'About being Esme?'

Esme smiles, her eyes locked on Iris's. 'You think they listen to me?'

Iris tries to meet her gaze but finds herself looking at the frayed neckline of the dress, the deep-set eyes, the fingers clutching the chair arms.

Esme leans towards her. 'You must excuse me,' she murmurs. 'I am not used to speaking so much. I have rather fallen out of the habit of late and now I find I cannot stop. So,' she says, 'you must tell me. Kitty had children.'

'Yes,' Iris says, puzzled. 'One. My father. You . . . you didn't know?'

'Me? No.' Her eyes glitter as they move about the dim room. 'I have, as you can see, been away a long time.'

'He's dead,' Iris blurts out.

'Who?'

'My father. He died when I was very young.'

'And Kitty?'

The cigarette woman is still chanting Iris's name under her breath and somewhere the other woman is still talking about the tired man and the kettle. 'Kitty?' Iris repeats, distracted.

'She is . . .' Esme leans closer, passes her tongue over her lips '. . . alive?'

Iris wonders how to put it. 'Sort of,' she says cautiously.

'Sort of?'

'She has Alzheimer's.'

Esme stares at her. 'Alzheimer's?'

'It's a form of memory lo—'

'I know what Alzheimer's is.'

'Yes. Sorry.'

Esme sits for a moment, looking out of the window. 'They are closing this place, aren't they?' she says abruptly.

Iris hesitates, almost glances towards the nurses, then remembers she mustn't.

'They deny it,' Esme says, 'but it's true. Isn't it?'

Iris nods.

Esme reaches out and laces both her hands round one of Iris's. 'You have come to take me away,' she says, in an urgent voice. 'That is why you are here.'

Iris studies her face. Esme looks nothing like her grandmother. Can it really be possible that she and this woman are related? 'Esme, I didn't even know you existed until yesterday. I'd never even heard your name before. I would like to help you, I really would—'

'Is that why you are here? Tell me yes or no.'

'I will help you all I can—'

'Yes or no,' Esme repeats.

Iris swallows hard. 'No,' she says, 'I can't. I . . . I haven't had the chance to—'

But Esme is withdrawing her hands, turning her head away from her. And something about her changes, and Iris has to hold her breath because she has seen something passing over the woman's face, like a shadow cast on water. Iris stares, long after the impression has gone, long after Esme has got up and crossed the room and disappeared through one of the doors. Iris cannot believe it. In Esme's face, for a moment, she saw her father's.

'I don't get it,' Alex is saying from the other side of the counter. It's a Saturday lunchtime and he and Fran have dropped into the shop, bringing Iris an inedible sandwich from an overpriced delicatessen. 'I don't understand.'

'Alex, I've explained it to you four times now,' Iris says, leaning on the counter, fingering the thin pelt of a kid glove. Its softness is oddly distasteful and she shudders. 'How many more times do we have to go over it before it penetrates your skull that—'

'I think Alex just means that it's hard to comprehend, Iris,' Fran interjects in a soft voice. 'That there are a lot of issues to deal with here.'

Iris focuses briefly on her sister-in-law. She appears to be all one hue, a kind of pale fawn. Her hair, her skin, her clothes. She sits on one of the chairs Iris has stationed near the changing room, her legs crossed and – is this Iris's imagination? – her raincoat held about her. She doesn't like second-hand clothes. She told Iris this once. What if someone died in them, she said. So what if they did, Iris replied.

Alex is still going on about Euphemia Lennox. 'You're telling me that no one's ever heard of her?' he is saying. 'Not you, not your mum, not anyone?'

Iris sighs. 'Yes. That's exactly what I'm saying. Mum says that Dad was definitely under the impression that Grandma was an only one, and that Grandma used to refer to it frequently. The fact that she had no siblings.'

Alex takes an enormous bite of his own sandwich and speaks through it. 'Then who's to say these people haven't made a mistake?'

Iris turns the glove over in her hand. It has three mother-of-pearl buttons at the narrow wrist. 'They haven't. I saw her, Alex, she . . .' She stops herself, glancing towards Fran. Then she leans forward briefly, so that her forehead makes contact with the cool glass of the counter. 'There are papers,' she says, straightening up again. 'Legal papers. Incontrovertible evidence. She's who they say she is. Grandma has a sister, alive and well and in a madhouse.'

'It's so . . .' Fran takes a long time to search for the word she wants; she has to close her eyes with the effort of it. '. . . bizarre,' she comes up with eventually, pulling each and every vowel out of it. 'For that to happen in a family.

It's very . . . very . . .' She closes her eyes again, frowning, searching.

'Bizarre?' Iris supplies. It is a word for which she has a particular dislike.

'Yes.' Fran and Iris look at each other for a moment. Fran blinks. 'I don't mean that your family's bizarre, Iris, I just—'

'You don't know my family.'

Fran laughs. 'Well, I know Alex.' She reaches out to touch his sleeve but he is standing just a little too far away so that her hand falls into the space between them.

Iris says nothing. She wants to say: what would you know? She wants to say: I came all the way to bloody Connecticut for your wedding and not one of your family thought to address a single word to me, how's that for bizarre? She wants to say: I gave you possibly the most beautiful nineteen-sixties Scandinavian coatdress I have ever seen as a wedding present and I have never once seen you wear it.

Alex lets out a cough. Iris turns to look at him. There is a minute, imperceptible flex in his facial muscles, a twitching raise of an eyebrow, a slight downturn of the mouth.

'The question is,' Iris says, looking away again, 'what I'm going to do about it. Whether I—'

'Now, hang on,' Alex says, putting down his bottle of water, and Iris bristles at the imperative tone. 'This has nothing to do with you.'

'Alex, it does, it's—'

'It doesn't. She's, what, some distant relation of yours and—'

'My great-aunt,' Iris says. 'Not that distant.'

'Whatever. This is a mess made by someone else, by your grandmother, if anyone. It's nothing to do with you. You mustn't have anything more to do with it. Do you hear me? Iris? Promise me you won't.'

Iris's grandmother is sitting in a leather chair, her feet propped on a stool, a cardigan around her shoulders. Outside the window, an elderly man shuffles up and down the terrace, hands held behind his back.

Iris stands in the doorway. She doesn't come here very often. As a child, she was taken to visit her grandmother once a week. She had liked the gloomy old house, the overgrown garden. She used to run up and down the tangled, mossy paths, in and out of the gazebo. And her grandmother had liked having her there, in a pretty dress, to show her friends. 'My Iris,' she used to call her, 'my flower.' But, as a teenager, her grandmother lost enthusiasm for her. 'You look disgusting,' she said once, when Iris appeared in a skirt she had made herself, 'no decent man will have you if you make an exhibition of yourself like that.'

'She's just had her dinner,' the care assistant says, 'haven't you, Kathleen?'

Her grandmother looks up at the sound of her name but, seeing no one who means anything to her, looks down again at her lap.

'Hello,' Iris says. 'It's me, Iris.'

'Iris,' her grandmother repeats.

'Yes.'

'My son has a little girl called Iris.'

'That's right,' Iris says, 'that's—'

'Of course it's right,' her grandmother snaps. 'Do you think I'm a fool?'

Iris pulls up a stool and sits down, her bag on her lap. 'No. I don't. I just meant that that's me. I'm your son's daughter.'

Her grandmother looks at her, long and hard, her face unsure, almost frightened. 'Don't be ridiculous,' she says, and shuts her eyes.

Iris looks about her. Her grandmother's room is thickly carpeted, choked with antique furniture, and has a view over the garden. A fountain twists in the distance and it is possible to make out the roofs of the Old Town, a crane wheeling in the sky above the city. Beside the bed are two books and Iris is just tilting her head to see what they are when her grandmother opens her eyes. 'I'm waiting for someone to do up my cardigan,' she says.

'I'll do it,' Iris says.

'I'm cold.'

Iris stands up, leans over and reaches for the buttons.

'What are you doing?' her grandmother squawks, shrinking into the chair, batting at Iris's hands. 'What are you doing?'

'I was helping you with your cardigan.'

'Why?'

'You were cold.'

'Was I?'

'Yes.'

'That's because my cardigan isn't buttoned. I need it done up.'

Iris sits back and takes a deep breath. 'Grandma,' she says, 'I came today because I wanted to ask you about Esme.'

Her grandmother turns towards her, but seems to become distracted by a handkerchief poking out of her cuff.

'Do you remember Esme?' Iris persists. 'Your sister?'

Her grandmother plucks at the handkerchief and it unwinds from her sleeve, falling into her lap, and Iris half expects there to be a string of them, all knotted together.

'Did I have lunch?' her grandmother asks.

'Yes. You've had dinner too.'

'What did I have?'

'Beef,' Iris invents.

This makes her grandmother furious. 'Beef? Why are you talking about beef?' She swings round wildly to peer out of the door. 'Who are you? I don't know you.'

Iris suppresses a sigh and looks out at the fountain. 'I'm your granddaughter. My father was—'

'She wouldn't let go of the baby,' her grandmother says suddenly.

'Who?' Iris pounces. 'Esme?'

Her grandmother's eyes are focused somewhere beyond the window. 'They had to sedate her. She wouldn't let go.'

Iris tries to stay calm. 'Which baby? Do you mean your baby?'

'*The* baby,' her grandmother says crossly. She gestures desperately at something, at meaning. 'The baby. You know.'

'When was this?'

Her grandmother frowns and Iris tries not to panic. She knows she doesn't have long.

'Were you there,' Iris tries a different tack, 'when the thing with the baby happened?'

'I was waiting in a room. It wasn't my fault. They told me afterwards.'

'Who?' Iris asks. 'Who told you?'

'The people.'

'People?'

'The woman.' Her grandmother makes an indecipherable shape round her head. 'Two of them.'

'Two of what?'

Her grandmother looks vague. Iris can sense her sinking back into the quicksand.

'Who told you about Esme and the baby?' Iris speaks quickly, hoping to fit it all in before her grandmother loses herself again. 'Whose baby was it? Was it her baby? Is that why she was—'

'Have I had my dinner?' her grandmother says.

Someone at the front desk tells her where to go and Iris takes a turning into an ill-lit corridor with lights stretching out in a row. There is a sign above a door, Records, and through the distorted aquarium glass, she sees a big room, lined with shelves.

Inside, a man sits on a high stool with a file in front of him. Iris rests her hand on the counter. She experiences a spasm of doubt about this mission. Maybe Alex is right. Maybe she should just leave this alone. But the man behind the counter is looking at her expectantly.

'I was wondering . . .' she begins. 'I'm looking for records of admission. Peter Lasdun said I could come.'

The man readjusts his glasses and grimaces, as if hit by a sudden pain. 'Those records are confidential,' he says.

Iris fumbles in her bag. 'I've got a letter from him in here somewhere, proving I'm a relative.' She delves deeper, pushing aside her purse, some lipstick, keys, receipts. Where is the letter he faxed over to the shop this morning? Her fingers brush against a folded piece of paper and she pulls it out, triumphant. 'Here,' she says, pushing it towards the man. 'This is it.'

The man spends a long time perusing it and then Iris. 'When are you looking for?' he says eventually. 'What date?'

'The thing is,' Iris says, 'they aren't exactly sure. Nineteen thirties or forties.'

He gets down from his stool with a long sigh.

The volumes are enormous and weighty. Iris has to stand up to read them. A thick epidermis of dust has grown over the spine and the top edges of the pages. She opens one at random and the pages, yellowed and brittle, fall open at

May 1941. A woman called Amy is admitted by a Dr Wallis. Amy is a war widow and has suspected puerperal fever. She is brought in by her brother. He says she won't stop cleaning the house. There is no mention of the baby and Iris wonders what happened to it. Did it live? Did the brother look after it? Did the brother's wife? Did the brother have a wife? Did Amy get out again?

Iris flicks over a few more pages. A woman who was convinced that the wireless was somehow killing them all. A girl who kept wandering away from the house at night. A Lady somebody who kept attacking a particular servant. A Cockenzie fishwife who showed signs of libidinous and uncontrolled behaviour. A youngest daughter who eloped to Ireland with a legal clerk. Iris is just reading about a Jane who had had the temerity to take long, solitary walks and refuse offers of marriage, when she is overtaken by a violent sneeze once, twice, three, four times.

She sniffs and searches her pockets for a tissue. The records room seems oddly silent after her sneezes. She glances around. It is empty apart from the man behind the desk and another man peering closely at something on a blue-lit microfiche screen. It seems strange that all these women were once here, in this building, that they spent days and weeks and months under this vast roof. As Iris turns out her pockets, it occurs to her that perhaps some of them are still here, like Esme. Is Jane of the long walks somewhere within these walls? Or the eloping youngest daughter?

No tissue, of course. She looks back at the pile of admissions records. She really should get back to the shop. It could take her hours to find Esme in all this. Weeks. Peter Lasdun said on the phone that they were 'unable to identify the exact date of her admission'. Maybe Iris should ring him again. They must be able to find out. The sensible idea would be to get the date and then come back.

But Iris turns again to Jane and her long walks. She flips back through time. 1941, 1940, 1939, 1938. The Second World War begins and is swallowed, becoming just an idea, a threat in people's minds. The men are still in their homes, Hitler is a name in the papers, bombs, blitzes and concentration camps have never been heard of, winter becomes autumn, then summer, then spring. April yields to March, then February, and meanwhile Iris reads of refusals to speak, of unironed clothes, of arguments with neighbours, of hysteria, of unwashed dishes and unswept floors, of never wanting marital relations or wanting them too much or not enough or not in the right way or seeking them elsewhere. Of husbands at the end of their tethers, of parents unable to understand the women their daughters have become, of fathers who insist, over and over again, that she used to be such a lovely little thing. Daughters who just don't listen. Wives who one day pack a suitcase and leave the house, shutting the door behind them, and have to be tracked down and brought back.

And when Iris turns a page and finds the name Euphemia Lennox she almost keeps turning because it must be hours

58

now since she started this and she's so dumbstruck by it all that she has to check herself, to remind herself that this is why she is here. She smooths the ancient paper of Esme's admission form with the pads of her fingers.

Aged sixteen, is what she sees first. Then: *Insists on keeping her hair long.* Iris reads the whole document from beginning to end, then goes back and reads it again. It ends with: *Parents report finding her dancing before a mirror, dressed in her mother's clothes.*

Iris goes back to the shop. The dog is overjoyed to see her, as if she's been away a week, not just a few hours. She switches on the computer. She checks her email, opens one from her mother. *Iris, I've racked my brains again and again about your grandmother and I don't recall her ever mentioning a sister,* Sadie has written, *Are you sure they've got it right?* Iris replies, *Yes, I've told you, it's her.* And she asks how the weather is today in Brisbane. She replies to other emails, deletes some, ignores others, notes down the dates of certain jumble sales and auctions. She opens her accounts file.

But as she inputs the words *invoice* and *downpayment* and *outstanding* her concentration keeps slipping out from under her, because in some corner of her mind is the image of a room. It is late afternoon in this room and a girl is unpinning her hair. She is wearing a dress too large for her but the dress is beautiful, a creation in silk that she has looked at and longed for and now it is finally on her, around her. It clings to her legs and flows around her feet like water. She is humming, a tune about you and the night and the music, and as she hums, she moves about the room. Her body sways like a branch in the wind and her stockinged feet pass over the carpet very lightly. Her head is so full of the tune and the cool swish of silk that she doesn't hear the people coming up the stairs, she doesn't hear anything. She has no idea that in a minute or two the door will fly open and they will be standing there in the doorway, looking at her. She hears the music and she feels the dress. That is all. Her hands move about her like small birds.

Peter Lasdun is crossing Cauldstone car park, struggling to put on his mackintosh. A keen wind is coming in gusts off the Firth of Forth. He gets one arm in but the other sleeve flaps free, turning the coat inside out, the scarlet tartan lining waving in the salty air like a flag.

He is just wrestling it into submission when he hears someone calling his name. He turns into the wind and sees a woman hurrying towards him. He has to stare at her for a moment before he can place her. It's that Lennox woman, or Lockhart woman or whatever her name is, and she is accompanied by a monstrously large dog. Peter takes a step back. He doesn't like dogs.

'Can you tell me,' she says, as she bears down on him, 'what happens to her now? To people like her?'

Peter sighs. It is ten past the hour. His wife will be opening the oven door to check on his dinner. The aroma of meat juices and roasting vegetables will be filling the kitchen. His children, he hopes, are doing their homework in their rooms. He should be in the car, on the bypass, not trapped in a breezy car park by this woman. 'May I suggest you make another appointment—'

'I just want to ask one question, a quick question,' she flashes him a smile, revealing a row of nicely kept teeth, 'I won't delay you. I'll walk to your car with you.'

'Very well.' Peter gives up trying to put on his coat and lets it flap around his ankles.

'So, what happens to Esme now?'

'Esme?'

'Euphemia. Actually, you know . . .' She trails off and flashes him that smile again. 'Never mind. I mean Euphemia.'

Peter opens his car boot and lifts in his briefcase. 'Patients for whom no provisions have been made by relatives,' he can see the policy document before him and he reads the words aloud, 'become the responsibility of the state and will be rehoused accordingly.'

She frowns and it makes her lower lip pout slightly. 'What does that mean?'

'She'll be rehoused.' He slams the boot down and walks towards the car door. But the girl tags behind him.

'Where?'

'In a state establishment.'

'Another hospital?'

'No.' Peter sighs again. He knew this wouldn't be quick.

'Euphemia has been deemed eligible for discharge. She's successfully been through a Discharge Adjustment Programme and a Rehabilitation Schedule. She is on a waiting list at a home for the elderly. So she will be transferred there, I would imagine, as soon as a place becomes available.' Peter slides into the driver's seat and inserts his keys into the ignition. Surely that will be sufficient to get rid of her.

But no. She leans on the open car door and the hound sticks its muzzle in Peter's direction, sniffing. 'When will that be?' she asks.

He looks up at her and there is something about her – her persistence, her doggedness – that makes him feel particularly weary. 'You really want to know? It could be weeks. It could be months. You cannot imagine the pressure that such establishments are under. Insufficient finance, insufficient staff, not enough places to supply demand. Cauldstone is due to close in five weeks, Miss Lockhart, and were I to reveal to you that—'

'Isn't there anywhere else she can go in the meantime? She can't stay here. There must be somewhere else. I would . . . I just want to get her out of here.'

He fiddles with the rear-view mirror, tilting it forward then back, unable to get a satisfactory view. 'There have been instances of patients such as Euphemia going to temporary accommodation until such time as a more permanent placing can be found. But my professional opinion is that I wouldn't recommend it.'

'What do you mean, temporary accommodation?'

'A short-term housing scheme, a residential hostel. Somewhere like that.'

'How soon could that happen?'

He gives his car door a tug. He really has had enough now. Will this woman never leave him alone? 'As soon as we can find transportation,' he snaps.

'I'll take her,' she says, without hesitation. 'I'll drive her myself.'

Iris lies on her side, a book in her hand. Luke's arm is round her waist and she can feel his breath on the back of her neck. His wife is visiting her sister so Luke is staying the night for the first time. Iris doesn't usually permit men to remain in her bed overnight but Luke had happened to call while she had lots of customers so she didn't have the time or privacy to argue her case.

She turns a page. Luke strokes her arm, then presses an experimental kiss to her shoulder. Iris doesn't respond. He sighs, shifts closer.

'Luke,' Iris says, shrugging him off.

He starts to nuzzle her neck.

'Luke, I'm reading.'

'I can see that,' he mumbles.

She turns another page with a flick of her fingers. He is gripping her tighter.

'You know what it says here?' she says. 'That a man used

to be able to admit his daughter or wife to an asylum with just a signature from a GP.'

'Iris—'

'Imagine. You could get rid of your wife if you got fed up with her. You could get shot of your daughter if she wouldn't do as she was told.'

Luke makes a grab for the book. 'Will you stop reading that depressing tome and talk to me instead?'

She turns her head to look at him. 'Talk to you?'

He smiles. 'Talk. Or anything else that might take your fancy.'

She shuts the book, turns on to her back and looks up at the ceiling. Luke is smoothing her hair, pushing his face into her shoulder, his hands moving down her body. 'When was your first?' she asks suddenly. 'How old were you?'

'First what?'

'You know. Your first.'

He kisses her cheekbone, her temple, her brow. 'Do we have to talk about this now?'

'Yes.'

Luke sighs. 'OK. Her name was Jenny. I was seventeen. It was at a new-year party and it was at her parents' house. There. Will that do you?'

'Where?' Iris demands. 'Where in her parents' house?'

Luke starts to smile. 'Their bed.'

'Their bed?' she says, wrinkling her nose. 'I hope you had the decency to change the sheets.' She sits up and folds her arms. 'You know, I can't stop thinking about that place.'

'What place?'

'Cauldstone. Can you imagine being in a place like that for most of your life? I can't even begin to see what it would do to you, to be taken away when you're still a—'

Without warning, Luke seizes her and tips her sideways, crashing her into the mattress.

'There's only one thing,' he says, 'that's going to shut you up.' He is disappearing under the duvet, working his way down her body when his voice reaches her: 'Who was your first?'

She releases a strand of trapped hair from under her head, readjusts the pillow. 'Sorry,' she says. 'Confidential information.'

He lurches out from under the duvet. 'Come on.' He is outraged. 'Fair's fair. I told you.'

She shrugs, impassive.

He seizes her round the ribs. 'You have to tell me. Was it someone I know?'

'No.'

'Were you obscenely young?'

She shakes her head.

'Ridiculously old?'

'No.' Iris reaches out, touches the shade on the bedside light, then withdraws her hand again. She places it on the swell of Luke's biceps. She examines the skin there, the way the white of his shoulder meets the browner skin of his

arm. She thinks, my brother. She thinks, Alex. The desire
to tell flickers, resurges, then wanes. She cannot imagine
what Luke would say, how he would respond.

His hands are tight on her shoulders and he is still
insisting, 'Tell me, you have to tell me.'

Iris pulls away, letting her head fall back to the pillow.
'No, I don't,' she says.

They were casting off from Bombay. The boat was vibrating
and groaning beneath them and people were crowded along
the quay, waving flags and banners in the air. Esme held
her handkerchief between two fingers and watched it flap
and flutter in the breeze.

'Who are you waving at?' Kitty asked.

'No one.'

Esme turned towards her mother, standing next to her
at the rail. She had one hand raised, holding her hat firm.
Her skin had acquired a taut, stretched look, her eyes
seeming to press back into their sockets. Her wrist,
protruding from her lace cuff, was thin, the gold watchstrap round it loose. Something in Esme moved her to put
her hand on her mother's wrist, to touch that bone, to slide
a fingertip between the skin and the links in the watchstrap.

Her mother shifted from one foot to the other, turned
her head as if to see who was next to her, then turned it
back. She reached forward with a jerked movement, as if

on strings, gave Esme's fingers two quick pats, then removed them.

Kitty watched her go. Esme didn't. Esme fixed her eyes on the quay, on the flags, on the great bales of cloth that were being loaded on to the ship. Kitty put her arm through Esme's and Esme was glad of it, the warmth of it, and she laid her head against her sister's shoulder.

Two days later, the ship began to pitch, very slightly at first, and then to roll. Glasses slid along the tablecloths, soup slopped over the sides of bowls. Then the line of the horizon began to see-saw in the portholes and spray hurled itself at the glass. People hurried to their cabins, staggering and falling as the ship bucked beneath them.

Esme studied the map that had been pinned to the wall in the games room, their course plotted in a line of red. They were, she saw, in the middle of the Arabian Sea. She said these words to herself as she made her way back along the corridor, clutching the handrail for balance: 'Arabian', and 'sea', and 'squall'. 'Squall' was a good word. It was half-way between 'squawk' and 'all'. Half-way between 'shawl' and 'squeamish'. Or 'squat' and 'call'.

The crew were scurrying about the wet decks, shouting to each other. Everyone else had vanished. Esme was standing at the edge of the deserted ballroom when a steward, darting past, said, 'Don't you feel it?'

Esme turned. 'Feel what?'

'Ill. Seasick.'

She thought about it; she took an inventory of her whole

being, searching for signs of unease. But there was nothing. She felt shamefully, exuberantly healthy. 'No,' she said.

'You're lucky,' he said, hurrying on his way. 'It's a gift.'

Her parents' cabin door was locked and, pressing her ear to the wood, she heard sounds like coughing, someone weeping. In her own cabin, Kitty was crumpled on the bed and her face was deathly white.

'Kit,' Esme said, bending over her, and she was suddenly seized with the fear that her sister was ill, that her sister might die. She gripped her arm. 'Kit, it's me. Can you hear me?'

Kitty opened her eyes, gazed at Esme for a moment, then turned her face to the wall. 'I can't stand the sight of the sea,' she muttered.

Esme brought her water, read to her, rinsed out the bowl beside the bed. She hung a petticoat over the port-hole so that Kitty wouldn't have to see the wild, swinging angles of the sea. And when Kitty slept, Esme ventured out. The planked decks were deserted, the lounges and dining rooms empty. She learnt to lean into the angle of the pitch when the ship shifted beneath her like a horse taking a fence. She played quoits, hurling the rope circles one by one on to a pole. She liked to watch the foaming path left behind the ship, her elbows hooked over the railings, to watch the grey, crested waves that they had passed over. A steward might appear and drape a blanket round her shoulders.

In the second week, more people appeared. Esme met a

missionary couple returning to a place called Wells-next-the-Sea.

'It's next to the sea,' the lady said, and Esme smiled and thought she must remember that, to tell Kitty later. She saw them both glance at the black band round her arm, then look away. They told her about the huge beach that stretched out below the town and how Norfolk was full of houses made of pebbles. They had never been to Scotland, they said, but they had heard it was very beautiful. They bought her some lemonade and sat with her on deck-chairs while she drank it.

'My baby brother,' Esme found herself saying, as she swirled the ice in the bottom of the glass, 'died of typhoid.'

The lady put her hand to her throat, then rested it on Esme's arm. She said she was very sorry. Esme didn't mention that her *ayah* had also died, or that they had buried Hugo in the churchyard in the village and that this bothered her, that he was being left behind in India while they all went to Scotland, or that her mother hadn't spoken to her or looked at her since.

'I didn't die,' Esme said, because this still puzzled her, still kept her awake in her narrow bunk. 'Even though I was there.'

The man cleared his throat. He gazed out to the lumped, greenish line of what he'd told Esme was the coast of Africa. 'You will have been spared,' he said, 'for a purpose. A special purpose.'

Esme looked up from her empty glass and studied his

face in wonder. A purpose. She had a special purpose ahead of her. His dog-collar was startling white against the brown of his neck, his mouth set in a serious downturn. He said he would pray for her.

Esme's first sight of the place her parents called Home was the flatlands of Tilbury, emerging from a shadowy, dank October dawn. She and Kitty had been waiting up on deck, straining their eyes into the mist. They had been expecting the mountains, lochs and glens they had seen in the encyclopedia when they had looked up Scotland, and found this low, fogged marshland a disappointment.

The cold was astonishing. It seemed to flay the skin from their faces, to chill the flesh right down to the bone. When their father told them that it would get colder still, they simply did not believe him. On the train to Scotland – because it turned out that this was not Scotland, after all, just the edge of England – she and Kitty bumped against each other in the lavatory as they struggled to put on all the clothes they had, one on top of the other. Their mother held a handkerchief to her face all the way. Esme was wearing five dresses and two cardigans when they pulled into Edinburgh.

There must have been a car or a tram, Esme thinks, from Waverley, but this she doesn't remember. She recalls flashes of high, dark buildings, of veils of rain, of gas-lamps reflected on wet cobbles, but this may have been later. They were met at the door of a large stone house by a woman in an apron.

'Ocht,' she said to them, 'ocht,' and then something about coming away in. She touched their faces, Esme's and Kitty's, and their hair, talking on about bairns and bonny and lassies.

Esme thought for a moment that this was the grandmother but she saw that her mother gave this woman only the very tips of her fingers to shake.

The grandmother was waiting in the parlour. She had on a long black skirt that reached to the ground and she moved as if she was on wheels. Esme doesn't think she ever saw her feet. She proffered a cheek for her son to kiss, then surveyed Esme and Kitty through pince-nez.

'Ishbel,' she said to their mother, who was suddenly standing very erect and very alert on the hearthrug, 'something will have to be done about the clothes.'

That night, Esme and Kitty curled round each other in a big bed, their teeth chattering. Esme could have sworn that even her hair was feeling the cold. They lay for a while, waiting for the heat of the stone hot-water bottle to seep through their socks, listening to the sound of the house, to each other's breathing, to the clip-clop of a horse outside in the street.

Esme waited a moment, then uttered a single word into the dark: 'Ocht.'

Kitty exploded into giggles and Esme felt Kitty's head brush against her shoulder as she clutched her arm.

'Ocht,' Esme said, again and again, between spasms of laughter, 'ocht ocht ocht.'

The door opened and their father appeared. 'Be quiet,' he said, 'the pair of you. Your mother is trying to rest.'

—gathered the holly that afternoon in the Hermitage, with a kitchen knife. I wouldn't do it, I was scared of the spines tearing at my skin (I'd been soaking my hands in warm water and lemon for weeks, of course, everybody did). But she pulled it from me and said, don't be a goose, I'll do it. You'll tear your dress, I said, and Mother will be angry, but she didn't care. Esme never cared. And she did, tear it, I mean, and Mother was vexed with us both when we got back. You are responsible even if Esme isn't, she said to me, you are responsible because Esme isn't, and we'd have to take it with us on our next visit to Mrs MacPherson. Mrs Mac, she liked to be called, made the dress I wore that evening. It was the most beautiful frock imaginable. We had three fittings, for it had to be right, Mother said. White organdie with an orange-blossom trim, I was terrified the holly would rip at it so Esme carried it as we walked there, taking care on the ice because our shoes were thin. Her dress was strange: she wouldn't have the organdie, she wanted red, she said, crimson was the word she used. Velvet. I will have a crimson velvet, she said to Mrs Mac as she stood at the fire. You will not, Mother said from the sofa, you are the granddaughter of an advocate, not a saloon girl, and she was paying, you see, so Esme had to settle for a kind of burgundy taffeta. Wine, Mrs Mac called it, which I think made her feel—

—wine is kept in the cut-glass decanters on the table behind the sofa. A wedding present from an uncle. I liked them at first but they are a devil, excuse my French, to dust. One must use a small brush, an old, softened toothbrush or similar, to get into all the fissures. I would ideally like to be rid of them, give them to a younger family member, say, as a wedding gift, a fine present they would make, but he likes them there. He takes a glass at dinner, only one, two on a Saturday night, and I must fill it only half full because it needs to breathe, he said, and I said, I've never heard such nonsense in all my life, wine can't breathe, you dunderhead, this last part said under my breath, of course, because it doesn't do to—

—and Mother said she must cut her hair, all of it, to the chin. But Esme wouldn't have it. Mother got out the pudding bowl from the kitchen cupboard and what did Esme do but take it from her and hurl it, smash, to the floor. It's my hair, she shouted, and I'll do as I please. Well. Mother couldn't speak, she was that angry. You will wait until your father gets home, Mother said, and her voice was still as ice, just get out of my sight, go off to school. The bowl in pieces all over the stone flags. Mother tried to—

—I wasn't to go to school. It wasn't done, a girl my age. I was to stay and help with the house, to go on calls with Mother. It wouldn't be long, she said, before I was married myself. And then I'd have a house of my own. With looks

73

like yours, she said. So she took me about their acquaint-
ances and she and I went to tea and to golf parties and
church socials and suchlike and Mother would invite young
men to the house. There was a time when I wanted to take
a secretarial course. I thought I would have been good at
the typing and I could have answered the telephone, I had
a nice voice, I thought anyway, but Father maintained that
the right thing was—

—when I left I thought of the bed, our bed, empty, every
night. Don't get me wrong, I was happy to be married.
More than happy. And I had a beautiful house. But sometimes I wanted to go back, to lie in the bed we'd shared, I
wanted to be there on her side, where she'd always lain,
and look up at the ceiling but of course—

—what was it she found so funny about Mrs Mac? I forget.
There was something and Esme used always to try to bring
it into conversation while we were there. I used to have a
pain from trying not to laugh! It made Mother cross. You are
to behave, Esme, do you hear, she used to warn, as we arrived
at Mrs Mac's gate. Mrs Mac's mouth was always full of pins
and you had to stand on a low stool to be fitted. I loved it.
Esme hated it, of course. The standing still was harder for
her. It's never as nice as you imagine it's going to be, she said,
when she got her wine dress. I remember that. She was sitting
on the bed with the box before her and she held it up by
the waist. The seams aren't straight, she said, and I looked
and they weren't but I said, of course they are, they're fine,
and you should have seen the look she gave me—

—terribly cold, I am. Terribly. I have to say I am not entirely sure where I am. But I don't want anyone to know this so I shall sit tight and perhaps someone will—

—what I call a button. That was it. She loved that more than anything and would put on the voice and pick up something, always something very ordinary, and say, now this is what I call a spoon, this is what I call a curtain, because Mrs Mac would look up at you as you stood there on the special stool and say, now, in here I'll put what I call a button. It used to make Mother so cross because we would both laugh and laugh. Don't mock those less fortunate than yourselves, she would say, with her mouth pursed. But Esme loved the way Mrs Mac said it and I always knew that she was waiting for it, every time we went there, and it used to make me very—

—someone in the room. There is someone in the room. A woman in a white blouse. She is pulling the curtains shut. Who are you, I say, and she turns. I'm your nurse, she says, now go to sleep. I look at the window. What I call a window, I say, and I laugh and—

When Iris arrives at Cauldstone, the social worker or Key Worker or whatever she is, is waiting for her in the lobby. An orderly leads them down a corridor. They enter a room and Esme is standing at a counter, a curled fist resting on its surface. She turns sharply and looks Iris up and down. 'They are fetching my box,' she says.

No hello, Iris thinks, no how are you, no thanks for coming to get me. Nothing. Was there, she wonders, a flicker of recognition? Does Esme know who she is? She has no idea. 'Your box?' Iris asks.

'Admissions box,' the orderly chips in. 'All the stuff she had with her when she came in. However long ago that was. How long has it been, Euphemia?'

'Sixty-one years, five months, four days,' Esme incants, in a clear, staccato voice.

The orderly chuckles like someone whose pet has just performed a favourite trick. 'She keeps a record every day, don't you, Euphemia?' She shakes her head, then drops her voice to a whisper. 'Between you and me,' she mutters to Iris, 'they'll be lucky if they find it. God knows what's in there. She hasn't shut up about it all morning. I'm surprised she remembers anything at all, the amount of—'

The orderly breaks off. A man in an overall has appeared, carrying a dented tin box.

'Wonders will never cease.' The orderly laughs and nudges Iris.

Iris stands and goes over to Esme's side. Esme is fumbling with the lock. Iris reaches out and pushes back the catch and Esme lifts the lid. There is a musty smell, like old books, and Esme puts her hand down into the box. Iris watches as she pulls out a brown lace-up shoe, the leather split and curled, an indeterminate article of clothing in faded blue check, a handkerchief with the initial E in uneven chainstitch, a tortoiseshell comb, a watch.

Esme picks up every item, holds it for a second, then discards it. She works quickly, intently, ignoring both Iris and the orderly. Iris has to bend to pick up the watch when it falls to the floor and she sees that its hands are frozen at ten past twelve. She is wondering whether it was midday or midnight, when she sees Esme peer into the depths of the box, then glance again at the discarded things.

'What is it?' Iris asks.

Esme falls on the heap and starts searching through it, flinging things aside.

'What are you looking for?' Iris asks. She offers her the watch. 'Is it this?'

Esme looks up, sees the watch in Iris's outstretched hand and shakes her head. She holds up the blue check material and Iris sees that it is a dress, a woollen dress, that it's crumpled and two of the buttons are missing, torn out from the fabric. Esme is shaking it, as if something might be caught in its folds, then casts it aside.

'It's not here,' she says. She looks, first at Iris, then at the orderly, then at the social worker, then at the man who brought the box. 'It's not here,' she repeats.

'What?' Iris says. 'What isn't there?'

'There must be another box,' Esme appeals to the man. 'Will you look for me?'

'There's just the one,' the man says. 'No more.'

'There must be. Are you sure? Will you check?'

The man shakes his head. 'Just the one,' he repeats.

Iris sees that Esme is near tears. She stretches out and touches her arm. 'What is it you're missing?' she asks.

Esme is breathing deeply. 'A length of . . . of cloth,' she holds her hands apart, as if imagining it between them, 'green . . . maybe wool.'

The four of them stare at her for a moment. The orderly makes a small, impatient noise; the man turns to leave.

Iris says, 'Are you sure it's not here?' She goes over to the box and looks into it. Then she picks up the fallen things one by one. Esme watches her and her expression is so hopeful, so desperate, that Iris cannot bear it when she realises that there is indeed no green cloth here.

Esme sits on a chair, shoulders slumped, staring into the middle distance as Iris signs a form, as the orderly gives her the address of the hostel to which she has agreed to drive Esme, as the social worker tells Esme that she will come and visit her in a couple of days to see how she's getting along, as Iris folds the blue check dress and wraps the single shoe, the handkerchief and the watch into it.

As she steps out into the sunshine with Esme, she turns to her. Esme is drawing the back of her hand across her cheek. It is a weary, resigned movement. She isn't looking at the sun or the trees or the driveway ahead of them. The tortoiseshell comb is gripped in her hand. At the bottom of the steps, she turns to Iris, her face full of confusion. 'They said it would be there. They promised they would put it in there for me.'

'I'm sorry,' Iris says, because she doesn't know what else to say.

'I wanted it,' she says. 'I just wanted it. And they promised.'

Esme leans forward to touch the dashboard. It is hot with the sun and vibrates slightly. The car goes over the humps in the driveway and she is thrown up then down in her seat.

She twists round suddenly. Cauldstone is being pulled away from her, as if reeled in on a string. The yellow walls look dirty and smudged from this distance and the windows reflect nothing but sky. Tiny figures toil back and forth in its shadow.

Esme turns back. She looks at the woman driving the car. She has hair cropped in at the neck, a silver ring on her thumb, a short skirt and red shoes that tie round her ankles. She is frowning and biting the inside of her cheek.

'You are Iris,' Esme says. She knows but she has to be sure. This person looks so oddly like Esme's mother, after all.

The woman glances at her and her expression is – what? Angry? No. Worried, maybe. Esme wonders what she is worried about. She thinks about asking her, but doesn't.

'Yes,' the woman says. 'That's right.'

Iris, Iris. Esme says the word to herself, forming the shapes inside her mouth. It's a gentle word, secret almost, she hardly needs to move her tongue at all. She thinks of blue-purple petals, the muscular ring of an eye.

The woman is speaking again. 'I'm Kitty's granddaughter. I came to see you the other—'

'Yes, yes, I know.'

Esme shuts her eyes, taps out three sets of three on her left hand, scans her mind for something to save her, but finds nothing. She opens her eyes again to light, to a lake, to the ducks and swans, right up close, so close that she feels if she leant out of the car she might be able to run her hand over their sleek wings, skim the surface of the cool lake water.

'Have you been out at all?' the woman is asking. 'I mean, since you went into—'

'No,' Esme says. She turns over the comb in her hand. You can see, from the back of it, the way the stones are glued into small holes in the tortoiseshell. She'd forgotten that.

'Never? In all that time?'

Esme turns it back, the right way up. 'There was no pass allocation for my ward,' she says. 'Where are we going?'

The woman shifts in her seat. Iris. Fiddles with a mirror suspended from the roof of the car. Her fingernails, Esme sees, are painted the emerald green of a beetle's wingcase.

'I'm taking you to a residential hostel. You won't be there for long. Just until they've found a place for you at a care home.'

'I'm leaving Cauldstone.'

'Yes.'

Esme knows this. She has known this for a while. But she didn't think it would happen. 'What is a residential hostel?'

'It's like . . . It's a place to sleep. To . . . to live. There'll
be lots of other women there.'

'Is it like Cauldstone?'

'No, no. Not at all.'

Esme sits back, rearranges her bag on her lap, looks out
of the window at a tree with leaves so red it is as if they
are on fire. She has a quick shuffle through things in her
head. The garden, Kitty, the boat, the minister, their grandmother, that handkerchief. Their grandmother, she decides,
and the department store.

Their grandmother had said she would take them into
town. The preparation for this expedition takes up most of
the morning. Esme is ready after breakfast but it seems her
grandmother has letters she must write, then she needs to
consult with the maid about tea, then the threat of a
headache casts a shadow over the whole outing, a tincture
must be made and allowed to draw, then consumed, and
the effect waited upon. Ishbel is 'resting', their grandmother
has told them, and they must be 'quiet as mice'. Esme and
Kitty have walked up and down the paths in the garden
until they were so cold they could no longer feel their feet,
they have tidied their room, they have brushed each other's
hair, a hundred strokes each, as directed by their grandmother, they have done everything they could think of.
Esme has suggested a clandestine visit to the upper floors
– she has spied a staircase going up and she has heard the
maid talking about an attic – but Kitty, after some thought,
said no. So now Esme sits slumped at the piano, sounding

out some minor scales with one hand. Kitty, in an armchair beside her, begs her to stop. 'Play something nice, Es. Play the one that goes daa-dum.'

Esme smiles, straightens her back, raises her hands and brings them down in the first, emphatic chord of Chopin's Scherzo in B flat minor. 'I don't think we're ever going,' she says, during a rest, timing it with a nod.

'Don't say that,' Kitty moans. 'We will. I heard Grandma say she couldn't bear the shame of people seeing us dressed like beggars.'

Esme snorts. 'The shame, indeed,' she mutters, as she brings her fingers down into the crashing chords. 'I'm not sure I'm going to like Edinburgh if it's considered shameful not to own a coat. Maybe we should run away to the Continent. Paris, perhaps, or—'

'We might never leave this house,' Kitty says, 'let alone get to—'

The door flies open. Their grandmother stands on the threshold, resplendent in a fur-trimmed coat, a capacious bag gripped in one hand. 'What,' she demands, 'is that dreadful racket?'

'It's Chopin, Grandma,' Esme says.

'It sounds like the Devil himself coming down the chimney. I won't have such a noise in my house, do you hear me? And your poor mother is trying to rest. Now, get yourselves ready, girls. We are leaving in five minutes.'

Their grandmother walks at a fair clip. Kitty and Esme have to break into a trot to keep up. All the way she mutters under her breath, about the various neighbours they pass, that the sky looks like rain, the pity that Ishbel couldn't come with them, the tragedy of losing a son, the paucity of the clothing Ishbel has provided for them.

At the tram stop, she turns to look them over. She gives a gasp and clutches her throat, as if Esme has come out naked. 'Where is your hat, child?'

Esme's hands fly to her head, feel the spring of her hair. 'I . . . I don't . . .' She glances at Kitty for help and notices with amazement that her sister is wearing a grey beret. Where did she get it from and how did she know to wear it?

Their grandmother lets out an immense sigh. She turns her eyes up to the sky and mutters to someone or something about trials and crosses to bear.

They are taken to Jenners of Princes Street. A man in a top hat holds the door for them and enquires, 'Which department, madam?' Mannequins waltz and twirl in the aisles and a shopgirl accompanies them across the floor. Esme tips her face back and sees balcony upon balcony, stacked on top of each other like the quoits on the ship. In the lift, Kitty feels for Esme's hand and squeezes it as the doors open.

The paraphernalia is astounding. They are girls who have spent their lives in nothing more than a cotton dress, and here are liberty bodices, vests, stockings, socks, skirts, under-skirts, kilts, Fair Isle sweaters, blouses, hats, scarves, coats, gaberdines, all, seemingly, intended to be worn at once. Esme picks up woollen combinations and asks where they go in the baffling order of things. The shopgirl looks at their grandmother who shakes her head.

'They are from the colonies,' she says.

'Sign here.' The man behind the reinforced-glass screen of the hostel counter pushes a registration book towards her and gestures at a pen.

Iris picks it up but hesitates, nib poised above the book. 'Shouldn't it be her?' she says, through the screen.

'What?'

'I said, shouldn't it be her?' Iris points at Esme, who is sitting on a plastic chair by the door, a hand gripping each knee. 'She's the one who's staying – shouldn't it be her signature?'

The man yawns and shakes his newspaper. 'Same difference.'

Iris examines the scrawls in the book, and the pen, which is held to the wall by a chain. From out of the corner of her eye, she can see a teenaged girl, slumped on another chair. She is bent in concentration over something, her hair hiding her face. Iris looks more closely. With one hand, the girl holds a biro and on the other arm she is circling every mole, every mark, every bruise in blue ink. Iris looks away. She clears her throat. She is finding it hard to think straight. She knows she needs to ask something, get some kind of clarification, but has no idea where to begin. She has an overpowering urge to call Alex. She would just like to hear him speak, to say to him, I am here in this hostel and what should I do?

'Er . . . I . . .' Iris begins. She puts down the pen. She wonders what she is about to say. 'Can we see the room?' is what comes out.

'What room?'

'The room,' Iris repeats, gaining conviction now. 'Where she'll be sleeping.'

The man lets the newspaper drop to his lap. 'The room?' he raps out. 'You want to see the room? Hey!' He is leaning back in his chair, calling to someone, 'Hey! There's a lassie out here wants to see the room before she signs in!'

There's a gale of laughter and a woman's head appears round the door.

'What do you think this is?' the man says. 'The Ritz?'

There is more laughter but then, without warning, he stops laughing, leans forward over the desk and barks: 'You!'

Iris jumps, startled.

'You!' He stands up now and raps on the reinforced-glass screen. 'You're banned. Get out.'

Iris turns to see a woman with a head of heavy, bleached hair and a grimy bomber jacket sidling past the desk, her hands deep in her pockets.

'You know the rules,' the man is shouting. 'No needles. It says that on the door, plain as day. So get out.'

The woman eyeballs the man for a long moment, then erupts like a roman candle, gesticulating, shrieking a long and voluble string of curses. The man is unmoved. He sits down and raises his newspaper. The woman, with no recipient for her anger, turns on the teenager with the biro. 'The fuck are you laughing at?' she shouts.

The teenager shakes the hair out of her eyes and looks her up and down. 'Nothing,' she says, in a sing-song voice.

The woman steps forward. 'I asked you,' she says menacingly, 'what the fuck you are laughing at?'

The girl raises her chin. 'And I said, nothing. Or are you deaf as well as wasted?'

Iris glances across at Esme. Her face is turned to the wall, her hands over her ears. Iris has to step over the teenager's rucksack to get to her. And when she does, she takes her arm, picks up her bag and guides her out of the door.

Outside on the pavement, Iris is wondering what she has done, what she's going to do now, when Esme suddenly stops.

'It's OK,' Iris begins, 'it's OK, you don't—'

But she sees a strange expression steal over Esme's face. Esme is looking up at the sky, at the buildings, across the road. Her features are illuminated, rapt. She turns one way, then the other. 'I know where this is,' she exclaims. 'That's . . .' she turns again and points '. . . that's the Grassmarket, down there.'

'Yes.' Iris nods.

'And that way is the Royal Mile,' she says excitedly, 'and Princes Street. And there,' Esme turns again, 'is Arthur's Seat.'

'That's right.'

'I remember,' she murmurs. She has stopped smiling now. Her fingers grip the edges of her coat together. 'It's the same. But different.'

Iris and Esme sit in the car, which is parked at the side of a street. Esme is pushing the seatbelt into the lock, then releasing it, and every time she releases it, she lifts it close to her face, as if examining it for clues.

'Hospital,' Iris is saying, to the remarkably unhelpful woman at Directory Enquiries. 'Cauldstone Hospital, I think. Or "Psychiatric Hospital"? Try "psychiatric" . . . No? Have you tried just "Cauldstone"? . . . No, one word . . . Yes. C-A . . . No. D. For – for "damn" . . . Yes, I'll hold.'

Esme has abandoned the seatbelt and has pressed the hazard light button on the dashboard. The car is filled with a noise like crickets. This seems to delight Esme, who smiles, presses it again, switching it off, waits a moment, then switches it on again.

'Really?' Iris says. 'Well, could you try just "hospital"? . . . No, not any hospital. I need this one, specifically. Yes.' Iris feels incredibly hot. She is regretting the jumper under her coat. She reaches out and covers the hazard button with one hand. 'Could you please not do that?' she says to Esme, then has to say, 'No, no, I didn't mean you,' to the Directory Enquiries woman who, magically, has managed to locate the whereabouts of Cauldstone on her system and is asking

Iris if she wants Admissions, Outpatients, General Enquiries or Daycare.

'General Enquiries,' Iris says, sitting up, enlivened now. This nightmare is nearly at an end. She will ask Cauldstone where she should take Esme next or, failing that, return her to them. Quite simple. She has more than done her duty. She hears the connection, a ringing and then a list of options. She presses a button, listens, presses another, listens again and, as she is listening, she realises that Esme has opened the door and is getting out of the car.

'Wait!' Iris shrieks. 'Where are you going?'

She shoves at her own door and stumbles from the car, still holding the phone to her ear – it seems to be saying something about how the offices are now shut, how the opening hours are between nine a.m. and five p.m. and that she must call back within those hours or leave a message after the tone.

Esme is walking speedily along the pavement, her head tipped back to look up. She stops at a pedestrian crossing, which is beeping, the green man flashing on and off, and stoops to peer at it.

'I'm in the Grassmarket with Es – with Euphemia Lennox,' Iris is saying in as calm and assertive a voice as she can muster while sprinting along a pavement. 'The hostel you sent us to is simply not satisfactory. She couldn't stay there. The place is completely unsuitable and full of – of— She can't stay there. I know this is my fault because I discharged her but,' she says, as she catches up with Esme, grabbing a fistful of her coat, 'I'd like someone to call me, please, as I'm bringing her back. Right now. Thank you. Goodbye.'

Iris hangs up, out of breath. 'Esme,' she says, 'get back in the car.'

They drive away from the Grassmarket, south, away from the centre, grinding their way through the rush-hour traffic. Esme sits in her seat, turning her head to see things as they pass: a churchyard, a man walking a dog, a supermarket, a woman with a pram, a cinema with a queue outside.

As Iris turns the car into the driveway for the hospital, Esme's head snaps round to look at her. 'This is—' She stops. 'This is Cauldstone.'

Iris swallows. 'Yes. I know. I . . . You couldn't stay at that hostel, you see,' she begins, 'so we—'

'But I thought I was leaving,' Esme says. 'You said I was leaving.'

Iris parks the car, pulls on the handbrake. She has to resist the urge to press her forehead against the steering-wheel. She imagines it would feel cool and smooth against her skin. 'I know I did. And you will. The problem is that—'

'You said.' Esme shuts her eyes, screws them up tight, bowing her head. 'You promised,' she says, almost inaudibly and, with her hands, she is crushing the material of her dress.

She won't get out. She will not. She will sit here, in this seat, in this car, and they'll have to drag her, like last time.

She breathes in and she breathes out and she listens to the shushing noise of it. But the girl walks round the front of the car, opens her door, reaches in to pick up the bag and she puts her hand on Esme's arm and the touch is gentle.

Esme releases her hold on her dress and she is interested in the way the material remains bunched up, pulled into peaks, even though her fingers have gone. The pressure on her arm is still there and it is still gentle and, despite it, despite everything, Esme knows the girl – this girl who has appeared from nowhere and after so long – has done her best. Esme does realise this and she wonders for a moment if there is a way to communicate it. Probably not.

And so she swings her legs sideways and, at the sound of the gravel under her feet, she finds she wants to cry. Which is curious. She pushes at the car door to shut it and that gets rid of the sensation – the satisfying clunk of it swinging to. She doesn't think she doesn't think she doesn't think anything at all as they walk up the steps and into the hall and there is the marble floor of the entrance hall again – black white black white black – and it is amazing that it is unchanged, and there is the drinking fountain with the green tiles, set into the wall, she'd forgotten that, how could she have forgotten that because she remembers now her father stooping to—

The girl is talking to the night porter and he is saying no. His mouth a round shape, his head swinging, back and forth. He is saying no. He is saying, not authorised. And the girl is gesturing. She looks tense, her shoulders hunched, her brow creased. And Esme sees what might be. She shuts her mouth, closes her throat, folds her hands over each other and she does the thing she has perfected. Her speciality. To absent yourself, to make yourself vanish. Ladies and gentlemen, behold. It is most important to keep yourself very still. Even breathing can remind them that you are there, so only very short, very shallow breaths. Just enough to stay alive. And no more. Then you must think yourself long. This is the tricky bit. Think yourself stretched and thin, beaten to transparency. Concentrate. Really concentrate. You need to attain a state so that your being, the bit of you that makes you what you are, that makes you stand out, three-dimensional in a room, can flow out from the top of your head, until, ladies and gentlemen, until it comes to pass that—

They are leaving. The girl is turning away. Iris, she is. The granddaughter, she is. She is picking up the bag by its straps, she is saying something to the night porter over her shoulder. Something rude, Esme thinks, something final, and Esme would like to cheer her for it because she has never liked the man. He turns off the common-room lights very early, too early, and sends them back to the wards, and Esme hates him for it and she would like to say something rude herself but she won't. Just in case. Because you never know.

And now they are walking back over the gravel towards the car, and this time Esme listens. She walks slowly. She wants to feel the prick, the push of every bit of gravel under her shoe. She wants to feel every scratch, every discomfort of this, her leaving walk.

—we never spoke of it again, of course. The son, the boy, that is, who died. Tragic, it was. We were told not to bring up the subject. Esme would persist in talking about him, though, would constantly say, do you remember this, do you remember that, Hugo this, Hugo that. And one day, at the lunch table, when she suddenly started reminiscing about the day he learnt to crawl, our grandmother brought the flat of her hand down on the table. Enough, she thundered. Father had to take Esme into his study. I have no idea what he said but when she came out she looked very pale of face, very agitated, her lips trembling and her arms folded. She never spoke of him again, even to me, because I said to her that night I didn't want to hear about him any more either. She was in the habit, you see, of talking about him when we were alone at night in bed. She seemed to take it the way she took everything: excessively hard. When really the one who was truly deserving of all our sympathy was Mother. I quite honestly don't know how Mother bore it, especially after all those other—

—and so I took hers. I did. And no one ever worked it out, so I suppose—

—and Esme started, then, to have these odd moments. Her 'turns', Mother called them. She's having one of her turns, she would say from across the room, just ignore her.

You would come upon her and she might be at the piano or the tea-table or at the window, because she always liked to sit at the window, and she was like a clockwork toy one might give to a child, the mechanism all wound down. Perfectly still, motionless, in fact. Barely breathing. She would be staring into space and I say staring when in actual fact she didn't seem to be looking at anything at all. You might speak to her, call her name, and she wouldn't hear you. It could make you feel quite peculiar, to look at her when she was like that. It was unnatural, our grandmother said, like someone possessed. And I have to say that I found myself beginning to agree with them. She was old enough to know better, after all. Kitty, for heaven's sake, Mother would say, rouse her out of it, will you? You had to touch her, shake her sometimes, quite roughly, before she'd come back. Mother told me to find out what it was that caused it and I did ask but of course I could never say because—

—and Esme insisted the blazer wasn't hers. I'd gone out to meet her from the tram, that was it, because she'd said she hadn't felt well at breakfast that morning, a headache or something, I don't know, she did look very white and her hair was loose down her back, who knows what had happened to all the pins she kept in it to keep it out of her face at school? I don't think she liked school very much. And she said it wasn't hers. It belonged to someone else. Well. I turned over the collar and said, look, here's your name, it is yours—

—because what she said was, I think about him. And I couldn't think who she meant. Him, I said, who? And she looked at me as if I'd said I didn't know her. Hugo, she said, as if it was obvious, as if I was supposed to follow the ins and outs of her thoughts, and I don't mind telling you that it was a shock to hear that name again after so long. She said to me, sometimes I go back there, in my mind, to the library, to when you were all away and I was in there with . . . and I had to stop her. Don't, I said, hush. Because I couldn't bear to hear it. I couldn't even bear to think of it. I had my hands over my ears. A horrible thing to dwell on. Three days she was there alone, they say, with— Anyway. It does no good to dwell on these things. I said that to her. And she turned her head to look out of the window and she said, but what if you can't help it? I didn't say anything. What could I have said? I was busy thinking, well, I can't tell Mother that so what am I going to say instead because lying is not in my nature at all, by the way, so—

—and Robert just shrugged. He had the little girl, Iris, on his shoulders at the time and she was laughing, trying to reach up for the chandelier, and I said, be careful, mind you don't bump her head. Part of me was, I admit, thinking of the chandelier. I'd just had it cleaned and it was such a bother getting a man in to take up the floorboards in the room above and lower it into a cloth. Ladders and brushes and youths in overalls clogging the hall for days. But he said, stop worrying, she's not made of glass. And I said, looking up at her because she is such a bonny thing, always has been, and she loves to visit me, always runs down the path, shouting, Grandma, Grandma. What an

idea, I said, made of glass indeed, who'd have thought—
—and she picked up the glass from the table and she threw it to the floor, smash. I sat tight on the chair. She stamped her foot, like Rumpelstiltskin, and shouted, I will not go, I will not, you can't make me, I hate him, I despise him. I didn't dare look down at the shards of glass on the carpet. Mother was so poised. She turned to the maid who was standing at the wall and said, would you help Miss Esme to another tumbler, please, then turned back to my father and—

Iris puts Esme's bag down next to the bed in the boxroom. She cannot quite believe that this is happening. The foreshadow of a headache is pressing down on her temples and she would like to go into the living room and lie down on the floor.

'You'll be OK in here,' she says, more to reassure herself than anyone else. 'It's a bit small. But it's only for a few nights. On Monday we'll get something else sorted. I'll ring the social worker and—' She stops because she realises Esme is speaking.

'– maid's room,' Esme is saying.

Iris is annoyed by this. 'Well, it's all there is,' she says crossly. Yes, the flat is small but she likes it and she is tempted to remind this person that her choices are limited to this servant's boxroom and the hostel from hell.

'It used to be green.'

Iris is shoving a chair back against the wall, pulling the duvet straight. 'What did?'

'The room.'

Iris stops fiddling with the duvet. She straightens up and looks at Esme, who is standing at the door, rubbing her palm over the handle.

'You lived here?' Iris says, aghast. 'In this house?'

'Yes,' Esme nods, touching the wall now, 'I did.'

'I . . . I had no idea.' Iris finds that she is inexplicably annoyed. 'Why didn't you say?'

'When?'

'When . . .' Iris gropes for what she is talking about, what she means. What does she mean? '. . . well,' she snaps, 'when we arrived.'

'You didn't ask.'

Iris takes a deep breath. She can't quite fathom how all this has come about: how it came to be that she has a forgotten, possibly deranged geriatric sleeping in her spare room. What is she going to do with her? How is she going to pass the time until Monday morning when she can get on to Cauldstone or Social Services or whoever and get something done? What if something terrible happens?

'This was the attic,' Esme is saying.

'Yes. That's right.' And Iris suddenly detests the inflection of her own voice. Its patronising emphasis as it concedes to the woman that, yes, this was once the attic of the house she grew up in, the house from which she was taken away. Iris drags frantically through her recollections of anything her grandmother might have said about that time. How is it possible that she never mentioned a sister?

'So, you lived here when you came back from India?' Iris says, at random.

'Well, it wasn't really coming back. Not for me and Kitty. We were born there.'

'Oh. Right.'

'But for my parents it was. Coming back, I mean.' Esme looks around the room again, touches the door frame.

'Kitty had the house converted into flats,' Iris begins, because she feels she owes this woman some kind of explanation. 'This one and two others – bigger ones. I can't remember when. She lived in the ground-floor flat for years. The whole lot was sold to pay for her care. Except this one, which she signed over to me. I used to visit her when I was little and the house was still a whole house then. It was huge. A big garden. Beautiful.' Iris realises that she is gabbling and stops.

'Yes, it was. My mother liked to garden.'

Iris tugs at a strand of hair over her eyes. She cannot fathom the strangeness of all this. She has acquired a relative. A relative who knows her home better than she does. 'Which was your room?' she asks.

Esme turns. She points. 'The floor below. The one overlooking the street. It was mine and Kitty's. We shared.'

Iris dials her brother's number. 'Alex, it's me.' She carries the telephone into the kitchen and kicks the door shut. 'Listen, she's here.'

'Who's where?' he says, and his voice sounds very near. 'And why are you whispering?'

'Esme Lennox.'

'Who?'

Iris sighs, exasperated. 'Do you ever listen to a word I say? Esme—'

'You mean the madwoman?' Alex raps out.

'Yes. She's here. In my flat.'

'How come?'

'Because . . .' Iris has to think about this. It's a good question. Why is she here? 'Because I couldn't leave her in the crack den.'

'What are you talking about?'

'The hostel.'

'What hostel?'

'Never mind. Look,' Iris presses her fingertips to her forehead and does a few circuits of the kitchen table, 'what am I going to do?'

There is a pause. In the background of Alex's office, she can hear the bleep of telephones, someone shouting something about an email. 'Iris, I don't get it,' Alex says. 'What is she doing in your flat?'

'I had to do something with her! There's nowhere else for her to go. What was I supposed to do?'

'But it's ridiculous. She's not your responsibility. Get on to the council or something.'

'Al, I—'

'Is she dangerous?'

Iris is about to say no when she realises that she has no idea. She tries not to think about the words she saw upside-down in Lasdun's file. Bi-polar. Electro-convulsive. She looks about her. The knife rack on the wall, the gas-rings, the matches on the work surface. She turns her back, faces the blank wall. 'I . . . I don't think so.'

'You don't think so? Didn't you ask?'

'Well, no, I . . . I wasn't thinking straight.'

'Jesus Christ, Iris, you're harbouring a lunatic you know nothing about.'

Iris sighs. 'She's not a lunatic.'

'How long was she in that place?'

She sighs again. 'I don't know,' she mutters. 'Sixty years, something like that.'

'Iris, you don't get banged up for sixty years for nothing.' She hears someone in the office calling his name. 'Look,' he says, 'I have to go. I'll call you later, OK?'

'OK.' She hangs up and places both hands on the counter. She hears the creak of a floorboard, a light step, a throat being cleared. She lifts her head and glances again at the row of knives.

Iris wonders sometimes how she would explain Alex, if she needed to. How would she begin? Would she say, we grew up together? Would she say, but we're not related by blood? Would she say that in her bag she carries a pebble he gave her more than twenty years ago? And that he doesn't know this?

She could say that she first saw him when he was six and

she was five. That she has barely known life without him. That he came into her sights one day and has never left them since. That she can recall the first time she ever heard his name.

She was in the bath. Her mother was there, sitting on the floor in the bathroom, and they were talking about a girl in Iris's class at school, and in the middle of the conversation, which Iris had been enjoying, her mother suddenly asked if Iris remembered a man called George. He took them out the other week and he showed Iris how to fly a kite. Did she remember? Iris did, but didn't say so. And her mother then said that George would be moving into their flat next week and that she hoped Iris would like that, would like him. Her mother began to pour water over her shoulders, over her arms.

'Maybe,' her mother said, 'you'd like to call him Uncle George.'

Iris watched the streams of bathwater fork into tiny rivulets as it coursed over her skin. She squeezed her flannel between both hands until it was a hard, damp ball inside her palms.

'But he's not my uncle,' she said, as she sank the flannel into the hot water again.

'That's true.' Her mother sat back on her heels and reached for Iris's towel. Iris always had a red towel and her mother had a purple one. Iris was wondering what colour George would have when her mother cleared her throat.

'George is bringing his little boy with him. Alexander.

He's almost the same age as you. Won't that be nice? I thought you could help me clear out the spare room for him. Make it look welcoming. What do you think?'

Iris was watching from under the kitchen table when George and his son arrived. She had pulled the cloth down low and she sat cross-legged, waiting. In the folds of her skirt she had hidden three ginger snaps. In case George was late. Because she was not coming out for a long time. She told her mother this and her mother said, 'All right, sweetheart,' and carried on peeling carrots.

When the doorbell rang, Iris crammed two ginger snaps into her mouth. One in each cheek. Which left only one for emergencies but she didn't care. She heard her mother open the door, say hello with a funny emphasis, hel-*lo*, and then say, it's lovely to see you again, Alexander, come in, come in. Iris allowed herself one small chew. So she'd met him before?

Iris shunted herself down on to her stomach. From here, she could peer under the hem of the tablecloth, which gave her a clear view of the kitchen lino, the sofa, the door into the hall. And in that door appeared a man. He had sandy, wavy hair, a green jacket with patches on the elbows, and he was carrying a bunch of flowers. Nerines. Iris knew a lot about flowers. Her father had taught her.

She was thinking about this, about her walks round the garden with her father, when she saw the boy. Iris recognised him instantly. She had seen him before. She had seen lots of him before. On the walls of the Italian churches her mother had taken her to last summer, which were painted with pictures of angels. Angels, everywhere you looked. With wings and harps and flowing pieces of cloth. Alexander had the same wide blue gaze, the curling yellow hair, the delicate fingers. It had been in one of those churches that her mother had told her about her father. She said, Iris, your father died. She said, he loved you. She said, it was no one's fault. They had been sitting in the back pew of a church that had strange windows. They weren't glass but made of some gold-coloured stone that had, her mother told her, been cut very fine, so fine as to let the light through. 'Alabaster' was the word. They read it in the book her mother had in her bag. And after her mother had told her, she held Iris's hand, very tight, and Iris looked at these windows, the way the sunlight behind them made them glow like embers, and she looked at the angels on the walls, the wings stretched out, their faces turned upwards. Towards heaven, her mother said.

So Iris lay on her stomach, swallowing hard at the molten ginger in her throat, staring at the angel boy who had sat himself down on her sofa, as if he were just an ordinary mortal like the rest of them. Her mother and George disappeared into the corridor and then Iris heard them coming in and out of the front door, carrying bags and boxes and laughing to each other.

Iris pulled the tablecloth a fraction higher. She needed to get a proper look at this boy. He sat motionless, one sandal resting on the other. In his lap was a small knapsack and his hands were clenched round it. Iris tried to remember what her mother had said about him. That he was shy. That his mother had gone off and he hadn't seen her since. That he might be sad because of this. That he'd had chickenpox recently.

She watched as he looked at a drawing Iris had done of a sunset that her mother had taped to the wall. He looked away again quickly. He turned his head towards the window, then he turned it back.

On the crest of an impulse, Iris scrambled to her feet and burst out from under the tablecloth. The angel on the sofa started, terror flashing across his features, and Iris was shocked to see his angel-blue eyes swimming with tears. She frowned. She stood on one leg, then the other. She advanced towards him across the carpet. He was blinking to get rid of the tears and Iris wondered what to say to him. What do you say to an angel?

She ate the last ginger snap contemplatively, standing before him. When she'd finished, she put her thumb into her mouth, twirling a plait round one of her fingers. She examined his knapsack, his sandals, his shorts, his golden hair. Then she popped her thumb free of her mouth. 'Do you want to see some tadpoles?' she said.

When Iris is eleven and Alex twelve, George and her mother part ways. He has met someone else. He goes, and takes Alex with him. Iris's mother, Sadie, sometimes cries in her room when she thinks Iris isn't listening. Iris takes her cups of tea – she isn't sure what else to do – and Sadie jumps up from the bed, wiping her face hurriedly and saying how her hayfever is bad this year. Iris doesn't point out that hayfever doesn't usually affect people in January.

Iris doesn't cry but she sometimes stands in the room that had been Alex's with her fists balled and her eyes closed. It still smells of him. If she keeps them closed for a long time she can almost pretend that it hasn't happened, that he hasn't gone.

Within a fortnight, Alex is back. George's new woman is a bitch from hell, he says, and Iris notices that Sadie does not tell him off for swearing. Can he live with them? Iris claps her hands, shrieks yes. But Sadie isn't sure. She'll have to check with George. But she isn't talking to George. Which is, she says, a problem.

Alex calls his father and they have a long argument. Iris listens, sitting squashed into the same armchair with Alex as he shouts at his father. Alex stays. A week later George comes and takes him home. Alex comes back. George arrives again, in the car this time, and takes him away. Alex returns. George sends Alex to a boarding-school in the middle of the Highlands. Alex runs away, hitchhiking back to the city, turning up on Sadie's doorstep early in the morning. He is dragged back to the boarding-school. He escapes again. Sadie takes him in but warns him he must call his father. He doesn't. In the middle of the night, Iris wakes to find him beside her bed. He is dressed, his coat on, a bag beside him. He says he is going to run away to France and find his mother, who will let him live with her, he is sure. Will Iris come with him?

They get as far as Newcastle before the police catch up with them. They are driven all the way back to Edinburgh in a police car, which Iris finds incredibly exciting. Alex says they'll have to handcuff him if they are to get him into his father's house. The policeman driving the car says, you've caused enough trouble for one day, sonny. Alex leans his head on Iris's shoulder and falls asleep.

Sadie and George have a summit meeting in the City Art Gallery café. Head of the agenda: Alex. Everyone is terribly polite. The Stepmother from Hell sits at a table in the corner, eyeing Sadie. Sadie, Iris observes, has washed her hair and worn her blue dress with red contrast piping. George is having trouble keeping his eyes away from the low-cut, red-edged V at the front of the dress. In the opposite corner sit Iris and Alex. Half-way through Alex says, fuck this, and that he is going to look at the second-hand record shops on Cockburn Street. Iris says he has to stay. They'll just think you're running away again, she says.

It is agreed that Alex will be allowed to switch to a boarding-school in Edinburgh on the proviso that he studies well and doesn't run away again. In return, he can live during his holidays with Iris and Sadie. But he must sit down with his father and stepmother once a week to eat dinner, during which – and George turns a steely eye on his son – Alexander will be expected to conduct himself in a courteous and orderly fashion. As George is saying this Alex mutters, up your arse, and Iris has to swallow hard so as not to laugh. But she doesn't think anyone else heard.

So every Christmas, summer and Easter, Alex lives with them, in the windowless boxroom in their tenement flat in Newington. When he is sixteen and Iris is fifteen, Sadie says she thinks they are old enough and responsible enough to look after themselves for a while, and she goes off to Greece on a residential yoga course. They wave her off from the front door, and as her taxi disappears around the corner, turn to each other with glee.

It doesn't take long. The first night Sadie is away, they have locked all the doors, pulled down the blinds, turned up the stereo, defrosted all the food in the freezer, opened out the sofa-bed in the living room, piled their bedding on to it and they lie there under a duvet, watching an old film.

'Let's not go out again,' Alex says. 'Let's just stay here all week.'

'OK.' Iris settles herself deeper into the pillows. Their limbs knock together under the duvet. Alex is wearing pyjama bottoms. Iris is wearing the matching top.

The people onscreen are running up a mountainside that is a violent, radioactive shade of green when Alex reaches out. He takes Iris's hand. He lifts it. He places it slowly, very slowly, on his chest. Just above his heart. Iris can feel it jumping and jumping, as if it wants to be free. She keeps her eyes fixed on the screen. The people have reached the top of the hill and are pointing excitedly at a lake.

'That's my heart,' Alex says, without moving his eyes from the television. He has kept his hand over Iris's, pressing it down into his chest. His voice is even, conversational. 'But it's yours, really.' For a while longer they watch the people onscreen as they waltz through a meadow in strict formation. Then Alex moves towards her through the flickering dark and she turns to him and she finds that he is hesitating and she doesn't see any other option for them so she pulls him closer and then closer again.

Through the wall, Esme is stepping slowly and sedately from the door to the shelves and back again. She touches the doorhandle – a round brass knob, slightly dented and smaller than she remembers. Or perhaps the ones downstairs were bigger? It doesn't matter because it has the same frilled brass surround and this pleases her. She counts the frills – petals, perhaps, but a flower made of brass is an ugly anomaly, an oxymoron, maybe – and there are nine. Which is an altogether likeable number. Three threes exactly.

She is trying to remember the names of the maids who would have lived in this room, high up in the eaves of the house. She has not thought about this for years. If, indeed, she has ever thought about it. It seems ridiculous to be able to recall this but, to her astonishment, the names come. Maisie, Jean. Not, perhaps, in the right order. Martha. But come they do. It is like reception to a radio frequency. Janet. If you're in the right place at the right time, you can pick up the signal.

Esme changes course. She leaves the door and the brass

flower and goes to stand in the corner beside the lamp. She turns her head, first one way then the other. She wants to see what else she can tune in to.

When Iris wakes, she gazes for a while at the blind pulled down over her bedroom window. She plucks at the duvet. She twirls a strand of hair. She is wondering why there is a knot of unease in her stomach. She glances round the room: all as it should be. Her clothes are strewn on the floor and the chairs, her books are stacked on the shelves, her clock glows at her from the wall. Then she frowns. The kitchen knives are sitting on her chest of drawers, alongside her makeup and jewellery.

Iris sits bolt upright in bed, clutching the duvet to her chest. How could she have forgotten? Sleep can do that to you – erase the most important thing from your mind. Iris listens, straining for sound. Nothing. The hiss of plumbing, the jumbled murmur of a television in the flat below, a car outside in the street. Then Iris hears a strange scraping noise, quite close to her head. It stops for a moment, then begins again.

She puts one foot to the floor, then the other. She pulls on her dressing-gown. She tiptoes out of her bedroom, across the hallway and stops at the door of the boxroom. The sound is louder. Iris raises her hand, hesitates, then makes herself knock. The scraping stops abruptly. Silence. Iris knocks again, more loudly, with her knuckles. Again, silence. Then a couple of footfalls, then silence again. 'Esme?' Iris calls.

'Yes?' The answer is immediate and so clear that Iris realises that Esme is right behind the door.

Iris hesitates. 'Can I come in?'

There is a rapid shuffle of feet. 'Yes.'

Iris waits for Esme to open the door but nothing happens. She puts her hand on the doorknob and turns it slowly. 'Good morning,' she says, as she does so, hoping she sounds more upbeat than she feels. She has no idea what she will see behind the door.

Esme is standing in the middle of the room. She is fully dressed, her hair brushed and neatly clipped to one side. She is wearing her coat, for some reason, buttoned up to the neck. There is an armchair next to her and Iris realises that she must have been pushing it across the floor. The expression on her face, Iris is astonished to see, is one of absolute, abject terror. She is looking at her, Iris thinks, as if she is expecting Iris to strike her. Iris is so taken aback that she can't think what to say. She fiddles with her dressing-gown cord. 'Did you sleep all right?' she asks.

'Yes,' Esme replies, 'thank you.'

Her face is still full of fear, of uncertainty. One of her hands picks at a coat button. Does she know where she is? Iris wonders. Does she know who I am?

'You're . . .' Iris begins '. . . you left Cauldstone. You're in my flat. In Lauder Road.'

Esme frowns. 'I know. The attic. The maid's room.'

'Yes,' Iris says, relieved. 'Yes. We're going to find you somewhere else but . . . but today's Saturday so we can't do that yet but on Monday . . .' She trails away. She has just noticed that, arranged on the small table beside Esme's bed, is the row of ivory elephants from the living room. Has Esme been wandering about in the night, moving things around?

'On Monday?' Esme is prompting.

'I'll make some calls,' Iris says distractedly. She glances round the room, trying to work out what else might have been changed, but sees only a hairbrush lined up with a handkerchief, three kirby-grips, a toothbrush and the tortoiseshell comb. There is something very dignified about the way these items are arranged. It occurs to Iris that they might be the only things Esme owns.

She turns away. 'I'll make breakfast.'

In the kitchen, Iris fills the kettle, gets the butter out of the fridge, pushes bread into the toaster. It strikes her as peculiar that she is doing the things she always does, as if nothing is different. She just happens to have a mad old woman staying with her for the weekend. Iris has to turn round at one point to make sure she's really there. And there she is. Esme, the forgotten great-aunt, at her table, stroking the dog's head.

'Do you live alone?' she is saying.

Iris has to muffle a sigh. How has she got herself into this? 'Yes,' she replies.

'Completely alone?'

Iris sits at the table and hands Esme some toast on a plate. 'Well, there's the dog. But apart from him, yes, I live alone.'

Esme lays her hand quickly on the toast, then the plate, the table edge, the napkin. She looks over the table, at the marmalade, the butter, the mugs of tea as if she's never seen these things before. She picks up a knife and turns it over in her hand.

'I remember these,' she says. 'They came from Jenners, in a box with a velvet lining.'

'Did they?' Iris looks at the old, discoloured bone-handled knife. She has no idea how it came into her possession.

'And you work?' Esme says, as she spreads butter on her toast.

She is doing everything, Iris notices, with an odd kind of reverence. How mad is she? Iris wonders. How do you measure these things? 'Of course. I have my own business, these days.'

Esme looks up from her study of the marmalade-jar label. 'How marvellous,' she breathes.

Iris laughs, surprised. 'Well, I don't know about that. It doesn't seem very marvellous to me.'

'It doesn't?'

'No. Not always. I was a translator for a bit, for a big company in Glasgow, but I hated it. And then I travelled for a while, saw the world, you know, waitressing along the way. And then somehow I ended up doing my shop.'

Esme cuts her toast into small, geometric triangles. 'You're not married?' she says.

Iris shakes her head, her mouth full of crumbs. 'No.'

'You never married?'

'No.'

'And people don't mind?'

'What people?'

'Your family.'

Iris has to think about this. 'I don't know if my mother minds or not. I've never asked her.'

'Do you have lovers?'

Iris coughs and has to gulp at her tea.

Esme looks nonplussed. 'Is that an impolite question?' she asks.

'No . . . well, it can be. I don't mind you asking but some people might.' Iris swallows her tea. 'I do, yes . . . I have had . . . I do . . . yes.'

'And do you love them? These lovers?'

'Um.' Iris frowns and drops a crust on to the floor for the dog, who darts towards it, paws scrabbling on the lino. 'I . . . I don't know.' Iris pours herself more tea and tries to think. 'Actually, I do know. I loved some of them and I didn't love others.' She looks at Esme across the table and tries to imagine her at her own age. She'd have been fine-looking, with those cheekbones and those eyes, but by then she'd have spent half her life in an institution.

'There is a man at the moment,' Iris hears herself saying and she is amazed at herself for doing so because no one except Alex knows about Luke and she likes to keep it that way, 'but . . . it's complicated.'

'Oh,' Esme says, and stares at her, hard.

Iris averts her gaze. She stands, brushing the crumbs off her dressing-gown. She dumps the dirty plates on the draining-board. She sees by the clock on the oven door that it's only nine a.m. There are twelve, possibly thirteen hours to fill before she can decently expect Esme to go to bed again. How is Iris going to occupy her for an entire weekend? What on earth is she going to do with her?

'So,' Iris says, turning back, 'I don't know what you would like to do today. Is there anything . . . ?'

Esme is looking at the bone-handled knife again, turning it over and over in her palm. Iris is hoping she might say something. She doesn't, of course.

'We could . . .' Iris tries to think '. . . go for a drive. If you like. Around the city. Or . . . a walk. Maybe you'd like to see some of the places you . . .' She loses conviction. Then she brightens with an idea. 'We could go and see your sister. Visiting hours start at—'

'The sea,' Esme says, putting down the knife. 'I would like to go to the sea.'

Esme propels herself through the water, breasting the dip and swell, her breath escaping in ragged gasps. She is beyond the breaking point of the waves, out in that queer, foamless no man's land. Around her legs, she feels the cold clutch of deep, powerful water.

She turns and looks back to land. The curve of Canty

Bay, the brown-yellow of the sand, her parents on a rug, her grandmother sitting bolt upright on a folding chair, Kitty standing beside them, looking along the beach, her hand shading her eyes. Her father, Esme sees, is making a gesture that means she should come further in. She pretends not to see.

A wave is coming, gathering its strength, drawing all the water around it towards itself. It moves at her, soundless, an impassive ridge in the ocean. Esme braces herself, then feels the delicious lift as the wave takes her, buoys her up, bears her towards the sky, then passes on, lowering her gently down. She watches, treading water, as it crashes and breaks, rushing in a frenzy of white towards the sand. Kitty is waving at someone and Esme sees that strands of her hair are escaping from her bathing cap.

They have taken a house in North Berwick for the summer. This is what people do, their grandmother told them. It is her job, she said, to see that Esme and Kitty are mixing with 'the right sort of folk'. They are taken to golfing lessons, which Esme detests beyond compare, to tea-dances at the Pavilion, to which Esme always ensures she brings a book, and every afternoon their grandmother gets them to dress in their best clothes and makes them walk up and down the sea front, saying how do you do to people. Especially families with sons. Esme refuses to go on these ridiculous walks. They make her feel like a horse at a show. Strangely, Kitty loves them. She spends hours getting ready, brushing her hair, patting cream into her face, threading ribbons into her gloves. Why are you doing that, Esme had asked yesterday, as Kitty sat before the mirror, pinching and pinching the skin of her cheeks. And Kitty had got up from the stool and walked from the room without replying. Her grandmother keeps announcing that Esme will never find a husband if she doesn't change her ways. Yesterday, when she said it at breakfast, Esme replied, good, and was sent to finish her meal in the kitchen.

Another wave comes, and another. Esme sees that her grandmother has got out her knitting, that her father is reading a newspaper. Kitty is talking to some people. A mother and her two sons, by the look of it. Esme frowns. She cannot understand what has happened to her sister. The sons are lumpish, large-handed, and hang back from Kitty's eager enquiries. She cannot imagine what Kitty is finding to say to them. She is just about to shout for her to come in to swim when something changes. The deep cold water beneath her is shifting, dragging at her legs. She is being sucked backwards very fast, the water around her rushing towards open sea. Esme makes an attempt to swim against it, back to the shore, but it's as if chains are tied to her limbs. There is a roaring sound like the moment before a storm. She turns.

Behind her is a green wall of water. The top of it is cresting, tipping over. She opens her mouth to scream but something heavy crashes on to her head. Esme is yanked under, dragged down. She can see nothing but a greenish blur and her mouth and lungs are filled with bitter water.

She flails this way and that but has no idea which direction is the surface, where she must fight towards. Something bangs her on the head, something unyielding and hard, making her teeth clash together, and she realises that she has hit the bottom, that she has been turned upside-down, like St Catherine in her wheel, but the sense of orientation lasts only for a second because she is flung forwards, downwards, dragged inside the muscle of the wave. Then she feels sand and stones grating against her stomach. She pushes hard with her hands and – miraculously – her head breaks the surface.

The light is white and jarring. She can hear the mourning cries of the gulls and her mother saying something about a gammon steak. Esme gulps at the air. She looks down and sees that she is kneeling in the shallows. Her bathing cap is gone and her hair sticks to her back in a wet rope. Tiny wavelets run past her to lap at the shore. There is a sharp pain in her forehead. Esme touches her fingers to it and when she looks at them, they are flecked with blood.

She stumbles to her feet. Angular pebbles press up into her soles. She almost trips but manages to stay upright. She lifts her head and looks towards the beach. Will they be angry? Will they say they told her to keep further in?

Her family are on the rug, passing round sandwiches and cuts of cold meat. Her grandmother's knitting needles work against each other, winding in the thread of wool. Her father has a handkerchief on his head. And there, sitting on the rug, is herself. There is Kitty, in her striped bathing-suit, her cap pulled down low, and there she is. Esme. Sitting next to Kitty, her sister, in her matching suit, accepting a cold chicken leg from her mother.

Esme stares. The scene seems to tremble and break apart. She has the sensation of being pulled strongly towards it, as if drawn by a magnet, as if she is still in the clutch of the wave, but she knows she is standing still, in the shallows of the sea. She presses her hand to her eyes and looks again.

She, or the person who resembles her, has her legs crossed. Her bathing-suit has the same snag on the shoulder, and Esme knows the way the rough wool of the blanket feels against bare skin, the way the spiked fingers of the marram grass behind them pokes through your clothes. She can, she realises, feel it at that very moment. But how can that be if she is standing in the sea?

She glances down, as though to reassure herself that she is still there, to check whether she has been exchanged in some way for someone else. A wave is passing, tiny and inconsequential, licking at her shins. And when she looks up again, the vision is gone.

If she is in the sea, what was she doing on the rug? Did she drown in the wave and, if she did, who was that person?

I'm here, she wants to shout, this is me.

And in her real-time life, she is there again. She is standing in Canty Bay. The sky is above her, the sand below her, and stretched out in front of her is the sea. The scene is very simple. It presents the fact of itself, ineluctable, unequivocal.

The sea is calm today, eerily so. Small green waves flop and turn at its edge, and further out the skin of it heaves and stretches as if, far below, something is stirring.

In a minute, Esme thinks, she will turn and look towards the land. But she hesitates because she is not sure what she will see. Will it be her family on the tartan travelling rug? Or will it be the girl, Iris, sitting on the sand, watching her? Will it be herself? And which self? It's hard to know.

Esme turns. The wind steals her hair, flipping it above her head, streaking it over her face. There is the girl, sitting as Esme knew she would be, in the sand, legs crossed. She is watching her with that slightly anxious frown of hers. But no, Esme is wrong. She is not watching her, she is looking past her, towards the horizon. She is, Esme sees, thinking of the lover.

This girl is remarkable to her. She is a marvel.

From all her family – her and Kitty and Hugo and all the other babies and her parents – from all of them, there is only this girl. She is the only one left. They have all narrowed down to this black-haired girl sitting on the sand, who has no idea that her hands and her eyes and the tilt of her head and the fall of her hair belong to Esme's mother. We are all, Esme decides, just vessels through which identities pass: we are lent features, gestures, habits, then we hand them on. Nothing is our own. We begin in the world as anagrams of our antecedents.

Esme turns back to the sea, to the keening of the gulls, to the rearing monster-head of the Bass Rock, which are the only unchanged things. She scuffs her feet in the sand, creating miniature valleys and mountain ranges. She would like, more than anything, to swim. People say you never forget. She would like to test this theory. She would like to immerse herself in the cold, immutable waters of the Firth of Forth. She would like to feel the ceaseless drag of the currents flexing beneath her. But she fears it may frighten the girl. Esme is frightening – this much she has learnt. Maybe she shall have to settle for removing her shoes.

Iris is watching Esme at the seashore when her mobile rings. 'LUKE' is flashing on the screen.

'Hi.'

'Iris?' he says. 'Is that you?'

'Yeah. How are you doing? Are you OK? You sound a bit odd.'

'I . . . I am a bit odd.'

She frowns. 'Sorry?'

'I think . . .' Luke sighs, and behind him she hears traffic, a horn blaring, and she realises that he has had to leave the flat to make this call. 'Look, I'm going to tell Gina. I'm going to tell her today.'

'Luke,' Iris sits forward on the rug, convulsed with panic, 'don't. Please don't.'

'I have to. I think I have to.'

'You don't. You don't have to. Luke, do not do it. At least, not today. Will you promise me?'

119

There is a silence on the line. Iris has to stop herself shouting, don't, don't do this.

'But I . . . I thought you'd . . .' His voice is tight, level. 'I thought you wanted us to be together.'

Iris starts to drag her fingertips through her hair. 'It's not that I don't want it,' she begins, wondering where she is going with this. For Luke to leave his wife would be a disaster. It is the very last thing she wants. 'It's just that . . .' she tries to think what to say '. . . I don't want you to leave her on my account.' Iris grinds to a halt. She is making frantic furrows in the sand in front of her. She listens to the silence at the other end of the phone. She can't even hear him breathing, just the roar and suck of traffic. 'Luke? Are you still there?'

He coughs. 'Uh-huh.'

'Look, this isn't a conversation we should have over the phone. I think we should talk about it properly, before you—'

'I've been trying to talk about it properly with you for days now.'

'I know, I—'

'Can I come over?'

'Um. No.'

She hears him sigh again. 'Iris, please. I can come right now and—'

'I'm not there. I'm at the sea with my great-aunt.'

'Your—' Luke stops. 'You mean the woman from Cauldstone?' he says, in a different tone.

'Yes.'

'Iris, what are you doing with her?' he barks out in his new, authoritative voice, and it makes her want to laugh. She can, for a moment, imagine what he's like in court. 'And what do you mean you're at the sea? Is anyone else with you?'

'Luke, relax, will you? It's fine.'

He takes a deep breath and she can tell that he is curbing his temper. 'Iris, this is serious. Is she there now? Why is she with you? I thought she was going into a home.'

Iris doesn't answer. There is silence on the line, punctuated by the drone of a motorbike in the distance. She glances around Canty Bay. The dog is some distance off, nosing a bank of seaweed. Esme is bending over, inspecting something in the sand.

'It's idiotic to have taken her on yourself,' Luke is saying. 'Idiotic. Iris, are you listening to me? You have this urge to give in to every wilful impulse that crosses your mind. It's no way to live your life. You have no concept of how stupid this is. Were you a trained professional, then perhaps, and I mean perhaps, you could see your way to—'

Iris blinks. For a moment, she can't catch up with herself. She is sitting in Canty Bay. Luke is still talking at her down the phone. The dog is staring at a seagull on a rock. And her aged relative is stepping into the sea, fully clothed.

'Esme!' Iris yells, struggling to her feet. 'Esme, no!' Then she says into the phone, 'Got to go,' and drops it. 'Esme!' she shouts again, setting off down the beach.

She doesn't know if Esme can hear her. Iris hurtles across the sand towards her. Is she going to swim out? Is she going to—

Iris arrives at the shoreline. Esme is stepping along the glassy, wet sand and tiny waves are breaking round her bare ankles. She holds her shoes in one hand and the hem of her skirt in the other.

'It's very interesting,' Esme says, 'don't you think, how it's the ninth wave that is the biggest, the most powerful. I've never understood the mechanics of it. Or maybe it isn't mechanics. Perhaps it's something other.'

Iris leans over, trying to catch her breath.

'Are you all right?' Esme asks.

The girl takes her to lunch in a café out on the far point of North Berwick. They sit outside on a planked platform and Iris mashes butter into Esme's baked potato for her. Esme is amused that she does this without asking, but she doesn't mind. Seagulls rip up the briny air with their cries.

'I used to come to the pool here when I was little,' Iris says, as she holds out the fork for Esme.

Again, Esme has to hide her smile. Then she sees that Iris is looking at the lines that criss-cross her arm and Esme takes the fork and turns her arm so that the lines, pursed white mouths, are facing the floor. She enters the zoetrope, briefly, catching a glimpse of Kitty on their swing in India, their mother lying on the bed in Lauder Road. But then she remembers she has to talk, to speak, and pulls herself out. 'Did you?' she says. 'I always wanted to, but we never did. My mother didn't approve of communal bathing.'

Esme looks at the blank stretch of concrete, which has been poured over the pool, then at the other tables. People eating, in the sunshine, on a Saturday. Is it possible for life to be this simple?

Iris is leaning over the table. 'What happened to you, in that place,' she is saying, 'in Cauldstone? What did they do to you?'

Her tone is kind, inquisitive. Esme does not blame her for asking. But she can feel herself wincing. Cauldstone and this place, this platform with the sea below it, do not go. How can she say these things here? How can she try to think them? She cannot even see them in a sentence. She wouldn't know how to begin.

Esme puts food into her mouth and she finds that, once she starts, she cannot stop. She pushes forkful after forkful of soft, warm potato between her teeth until her cheeks are packed and her tongue cannot move.

'We lived here for a while, after my father died,' Iris says.

Esme has to swallow once, twice before she can speak, and it hurts her throat. 'How did he die?' she asks.

'Oh, it was stupid. A stupid accident. He was in hospital for a routine operation and he was given a drug he was allergic to. He was young, only thirty-one.'

Esme gets flashes of this scene. She thinks she has seen this, or something like it. When? She can't recall. But she remembers the convulsions, the thrashing body, the lolling tongue, and then the awful stillness. She has to concentrate on her plate to get rid of them.

'That's very sad,' she says, and speaking the words is good because it distracts her mind into thinking about forming the syllables.

'My parents were already separated by the time he died so I didn't see him much, but I still miss him. It would have been his birthday next week.'

Iris pours water from a bottle into glasses for them and Esme is surprised to see tiny bubbles, thousands of them, rising to the surface, clinging to the sides. She picks up the glass and holds it close to her ear. There is the tiny crackling sound of the bubbles bursting. She puts it down when she sees Iris looking at her, alarm etched on her face.

'Which day?' Esme asks, to fill the gap, to reassure her.

'Sorry?' She still looks alarmed, but less so.

'Which day was your father's birthday?'

'The twenty-eighth.'

Esme is reaching for the water glass again but something stops her. She seems to see these numbers. The swan-like stroke of the two lined up close to the double circles of the eight. Switched around they make eighty-two. With another zero, they could be two hundred and eighty, eight hundred and twenty, two hundred and eight, eight hundred and two. They multiply and replicate in her mind, filling it to its edges, strings and strings of twos and eights.

She has to get up and walk to the barrier to get rid of

them and when she gets there she sees, below the planked deck where everyone is sitting in the sunshine, a mass of spiked, black rocks.

—realised that I have no idea when my parents' wedding anniversary is. I should have asked Mother. They didn't celebrate it, or not so as we knew. The wedding would have taken place in India, of course, Mother quite the colonial girl and Father just arrived. A wonderful reception party afterwards at the club. Everyone came. Everyone who was anyone. I have seen photos, Mother in a beautiful satin—

—and I took hers, it was as simple as that, but Father said I must never say, that—

—my husband bought it for me, or someone else did it for him, he paid for it anyway, and it must have been his idea. Very handsome, it was. A perfect circle of tiny, many-faced stones. It always caught the light in such a pretty way. Eternity rings are commonly given on the occasion of the birth of the first child, he said to me, and this was just as I was feeling very pleased and touched and, of course, that ruined the whole thing. That officious tone of his. He always liked to do things by the book. He kept a list in his desk of things like that. He would consult it. When to give paper and when to give gold, and so on and so forth and anyway—

—and we were taken to a studio in the New Town and they tried to get our hair looking the same, which, of course, was a thankless task because hers was wild, long, with curls all over: it could never have looked like mine. Mine would brush down nicely and sit well, close to my head. We had to pose for a long time, perfectly still. It was usual, I think, in portraits of siblings, for the elder to sit and the younger to stand behind. But because she was so much taller than me she was placed in the chair and I had to stand behind her with one hand resting on her shoulder and I always regretted that because I had spent all morning starching the pleats on the front of my dress and, of course, they weren't seen, being—

—that satin wedding dress made it back to Scotland with us. Mother let us try it on once. Esme went first because I wanted to do it, I wanted to try it on so badly that, when Mother asked which of us would go first, I could not speak. And when Esme stood before the mirror, she threw back her head and laughed and laughed. It was so short on her! She had such long legs, like a giraffe, and it did look very comical. But I couldn't laugh as well because I saw the set of Mother's face, saw that she did not like Esme laughing at her dress. I looked perfect in it. Mother said so. She and I were the same height. You can wear it on your wedding day, darling, Mother said. And Esme was standing behind us, I could see her in the mirror, and she said, not me, then? She was just being cheeky because, of course, there was no conceivable way she could have worn it and Mother snapped because Esme was in the habit of riling her—

—and when I heard the screaming I wound up my skip-ping-rope and I came running. She was all in a heap on the lawn, Mother and Father standing helplessly, staring down at her. Well, I was more used to it than they were. I put my arms round her and I said, what is it, tell me, what is it. What was it? I forget. There was always something, always some reason, however strange, with her, but you couldn't have guessed what it would be. You never knew, with her, what was going to happen from one minute to the next. I think that's why—

—and when the portrait came back, Mother gave word for Esme to be confined to her room all day. Esme looked so cross in it, her face glowering and furious. Mother had every right to be angry, of course. Well, with the price of the sitting and everything you could hardly blame her. And I was put out as well. I had spent an entire morning preparing my clothes, combing down my hair with water and rose oil so that it looked just so. And all for nothing. Mother said that no parent in their right mind would display a portrait like that. Esme was not at all contrite. The chair was so uncomfortable, she said, there were two springs digging into my leg. She was funny like that, always so ridiculously oversensitive. She was like that princess in the story about the pea and all the mattresses. Is there a pea, I would say to her when she thrashed about in the bed at night, trying to get comfortable, and she would say, whole pods of them—

—that ring Duncan gave me, I used to wear it. I wore it on my wedding finger, as is the custom with eternity rings.

127

But I can't see it. It's not there. I stretch out my hands in front of me, both of them, just to be sure. It's not there, I say to the girl, because there is always a girl. Never far away, watching you. I beg your pardon, she says, and I know it's not that she didn't hear me – I have a good speaking voice, very clear, I have often been told – it's that she's not listening. She is fiddling with some chart on the wall. My ring, I say loudly, to let her know that I mean business, they can be so flighty, these girls. Oh, she says and she still doesn't turn away from that chart, I wouldn't worry about that now, and this angers me so much I turn in my seat and I say—

—whole pods of them, as she wriggled about, trying to get comfortable, and it would make me laugh, and as soon as she saw me laughing, she would do it again and again. She always had that way, to make you laugh. Until, that is—

Esme stares at the spiked rocks. She stares and stares until they begin to lose their third dimension, until they begin to look unfamiliar, insubstantial. Like the way words said over and over become just a slurry of sound. She thinks of this. She says the word 'word' over and over in her head until she hears only 'dwur-dwur-dwur'. She is aware of those numbers, that two and the eight, trying to find a place to slip back in. They have been lurking at the edges where she pushed them and they are mounting an assault, a break-in. She won't have it. She will not. She slams all the doors, she throws the bolts, she turns the locks. She fastens her eyes on the rocks, the spiked crenellations of the rocks beneath the platform, and she scans her mind to find something else because the rocks and the word 'word' won't work for ever, she knows that. And suddenly she is rewarded because from nowhere she finds she is thinking about the blazer. She checks herself quickly. Can she think about this? And she decides yes.

The blazer, the blazer. She can recall the exact felted feel of it, the itchiness of its collar, the horrid embroidered crest on the pocket. She never liked school. The work she enjoyed, the lessons and the teachers. If only school could be just that. But the shoals of girls, forever combing and recombing their hair and snickering behind their hands. Insufferable, they were.

Esme turns away from the rocks. She is safe now. She keeps one hand on the wooden barrier, though. Just in case. She sees the rows of houses fitted together in a line along the beach road. She sees the girl, Iris, sitting with her legs crossed at the table, and it strikes Esme as odd that she herself had been sitting there too, just a moment ago. She sees the chair that had been hers — that is still hers. It is angled away from the table and there is her plate, with the half-eaten potato. Amazing how easy it is to get up and walk away from a table, from a plate of food, how no one stops you, how it wouldn't occur to anyone here that they could stop you.

She smiles at this thought. In some corner of her mind,

school is still ticking over. The giggling, the snickering, the laughter that happened behind her and would stop if she turned. She didn't care, she absolutely didn't. She wasn't interested in those girls and their grouse weekends, their coming-out balls, their notes from the prefects at the boys' school. She could lose herself in listening to the teachers, in knowing that her marks were good, better than anyone else's, almost. But there were days when she found the girls wearisome. Tell us about India, Esme, they would chant, pronouncing it 'In-di-ah', for reasons Esme never understood. And this only because she had once mistaken their questions as sincere and described for them the yellow mimosa dust, the iridescent wings of the dragonflies, the curved horns of the black-faced cattle. It had been several minutes before she realised that they were all stifling laughter in their jumper sleeves.

The laughter. Erupting behind her during lessons, following her like a dress train as she walked down a corridor. Esme could never really tell why, what it was about her that afforded them such hilarity. Does your hair curl naturally, they would ask, and then start giggling. Does your mother wear a sari? Do you eat curry at home? Who makes your clothes? When you leave school are you going to be an old maid like your sister?

That had done it. Esme had turned at that one. She had snatched up the protractor of Catriona McFarlane, high priestess of the tittering club, and pointed it at her like a divining rod. 'You know what you are, Catriona McFarlane?'

Esme had said. 'You are a sad creature. You are mean-spirited, soulless. You are going to die alone and lonely. Do you hear me?'

Catriona was astonished, her mouth slightly open, and before she could say anything else, Esme had turned away.

On the wooden decking, the girl Iris is shifting in her seat. A little uneasily. Has Esme been staring at her? She isn't sure. Two teacups, plumed with steam, have appeared on their table. Iris is sipping from one, holding it between both hands, which makes Esme smile because it is something her mother would never have allowed and Iris looks so like her: it is as if Esme has been given a vision of her mother in some idyllic afterlife, relaxing in the sunshine, with a new haircut, tilting a teacup towards her mouth with all expansive ten of her fingers. Esme smiles again and slaps the wooden barrier with her palm.

It was Catriona who switched the blazer. She is sure of it. And the only possible person who could have told was—

The girl is leaning forward in her chair, saying something, and the vision of Esme's mother enjoying a celestial cup of tea dissolves. It is just her and the girl, Iris, in a café by the sea, and all that was a long time ago. She must remember this.

But she is certain that it was Catriona. When Esme had got to the cloakroom that evening, it was jammed with girls pulling hats and coats off their pegs. As she had walked out into the corridor, she struggled to put on her blazer, pushing one arm down the sleeve and trying to find the other armhole.

It wasn't working. She couldn't find it. She put down her satchel and tried again but her fingers slipped on the lining, unable to find the opening. She will think later that at this point she saw, dimly, in the distance, Catriona flitting away along the corridor. Esme tore the blazer off her arm – horrible thing it was anyway, she didn't see why they had to wear them – and examined it. Had she picked up the right one? It looked the same, but then they all did. And there was her nametape, E. LENNOX, sewn into the collar. Esme hooked both arms into it and yanked it on to her back.

The effect was instantaneous. She could barely move, barely breathe. The felt of the blazer was stretched over her shoulders, pinioning her arms to her sides, nipping her armpits. The sleeves were too short, showing the bones of her wrists. It looked like her blazer, it said it was her blazer, but it wasn't. It wouldn't close over her chest. A pair of younger girls stared at her as they passed.

As Esme takes the seat at the table, Iris says, 'I ordered coffee for you but I don't know if you'd rather have tea.' She is gesturing towards the cup. Esme looks down at it. It is overflowing with white froth. A silver spoon sits in the curve of the saucer. And a small brown biscuit. Esme doesn't ordinarily drink either tea or coffee but thinks she will make an exception this time. She touches the fingertips of one hand to the scalding porcelain, then touches it with the other. 'No,' she says, 'coffee is fine.'

Kitty was waiting for her as she stamped down off the tram, leaning against the wall by the corner.

'What's the matter?' she'd said, as Esme approached.

'This isn't my damn blazer,' Esme muttered, without stopping.

'Don't swear.' Kitty tagged behind her. 'Are you sure it isn't yours? It looks like yours.'

'It isn't, I tell you. Some stupid girl has swapped it, I don't know—'

Kitty reached out and folded back the collar. 'It's got your name in it.'

'Look at it!' Esme stopped in the middle of the pavement and held out her arms. The sleeves reached just below her elbows. 'Of course it's not mine.'

'You've grown, that's all. You've grown so much recently.'

'It fitted me this morning.'

They turned into Lauder Road. The lamps had been lit, as they were at this time every day, and the lighter was passing on the other side of the street, his pole over his shoulder. Esme's sight seemed to close in at the sides and she thought she might faint.

'Oh,' she burst out. 'I hate this – I hate it.'

'What?'

'Just – this. I feel as though I'm waiting for something and I'm getting scared it might never come.'

Kitty stopped and stared at her, perplexed. 'What are you talking about?'

Esme lowered herself on to a garden wall, flinging her satchel to the ground, and looked up at the yellow flare of the gas-light. 'I'm not sure.'

Kitty scratched at the pavement with her toe. 'Listen, I came to tell you – Mr McFarlane's been to call. Mother's livid with you. He says . . . he says you put a curse on his daughter.'

Esme stared at her sister, then started to laugh.

'It's not funny, Esme. He was really angry. Mother says that when we get home you've to go to Father's study and wait for him there. Mr McFarlane said that you prophesied Catriona's death. He said you flew at her like a wildcat and put a curse on her.'

'A curse?' Esme wiped her eyes, still laughing. 'If only I could.'

After lunch, Iris and Esme wander away from the café, down the path towards the town. Wind bullies them from both sides and Iris shivers, buttoning her jacket. She sees that Esme bends herself into it, face first. There is something about her, Iris reflects, that isn't quite right. You wouldn't necessarily think she'd been locked up for her whole life, but there is something – a certain wide-eyed quality, her lack of inhibition, perhaps – that marks her out from other people.

'Ha,' she is saying, with a grin, 'it's a long time since I felt wind like that.'

They pass by a ruin, bedded into the grass like old teeth. Esme stops to look at it.

'It's an old abbey,' Iris says, poking at a low, crumbling

wall with her toe. Then, remembering something she'd read once, she says, 'The Devil is supposed to have appeared here to a congregation of witches and told them how to cast a spell to drown the King.'

Esme turns to her. 'Is that so?'

Iris is a little taken aback by her intensity. 'Well,' she dissembles, 'it was what one of them claimed.'

'But why would she say it if it wasn't true?'

Iris has to think for a moment, wondering how to put it. 'I think,' she begins carefully, 'that thumbscrews can make you pretty inventive.'

'Oh,' Esme says. 'They were tortured, you mean?'

Iris clears her throat, which makes her cough. Why had she begun this conversation? What had possessed her? 'I think so,' she mumbles, 'yes.'

Esme walks along beside one of the walls, putting one foot in front of the other in a deliberate, rhythmic fashion, like a marionette. At a cornerstone, she stops. 'What happened to them?' she asks.

'Er . . .' Iris looks around wildly for something to distract Esme. 'I'm not sure.' She gestures extravagantly out to sea. 'Look! Boats! Shall we go and see?'

'Were they put to death?' Esme persists.

'I . . . um . . . possibly.' Iris scratches her head. 'Do you want to go and see the boats? Or an ice-cream. Would you like an ice-cream?'

Esme straightens up, weighing the pebble in her palm. 'No,' she says. 'Were they burnt or strangled? Witches were strangled to death in parts of Scotland, weren't they? Or buried alive.'

Iris has to resist an urge to cover her face with her hands. Instead she takes Esme by the arm and leads her away from the abbey. 'Maybe we should head home. What do you think?'

Esme nods. 'Very well.'

Iris walks carefully, plotting their route back to the car in her head, taking care to avoid any further historical sites.

—a word for it, I know there is. I know it. I knew it yesterday. It is a strange thing, suspended from the ceiling, a frame of wire over which is stretched a purple fabric. There is a light inside it, hanging inside it. A switch on the wall will illuminate it when it gets dark. But what is the word for it? I am sure I know it, I can almost see it, it begins with—

—leen, Kathleen. There is a woman bending over me, too close to me, she is holding a wooden spoon. The spoon is dressed in a skirt and apron, with strands of wool stuck on in the place of hair, a face inked in with a huge red smile. It is a grotesque thing, a horrible thing, and why is she putting it in my lap? Everyone, I now see, has been given one and I do not know why. There is nothing for it but to dash it to the floor. The spoon's skirt flips up over its head and I see its single, pale limb as I—

—so Mother stopped at the corner, made her go back to the house to fetch her gloves. You always had to wear a pair of gloves in those days when out, it didn't do to be bare-handed, especially coming from a family like ours. Leather ones, fitted to your hands, everyone knew their size. She had exceptionally long fingers, the man at the glove counter in Maule's told us. An octave and two, she replied, with a smile, is my stretch. He had no idea what she was talking about. She was a good pianist but too undisciplined, our grandmother said. But Mother sent her back for the gloves and to fix her stocking, which had slipped down her leg, showing the skin between her hem and the stocking top, which, of course, wouldn't do. I went with her when I saw the thunderclouds in her face. I can't stand it, I can't stand it, she hissed to me, as we walked, and she was walking faster than usual so I had almost to run to keep up. These rules, these ridiculous rules, how is anyone supposed to remember them all? It's only a pair of gloves, I said, I did remind you as we were leaving the house. But she was furious, always chafing at the bit, she was. And we couldn't find the gloves, of course. Or we could find only one. I forget. I know we looked everywhere. I can't think of everything, I said to her, as we searched, because she was forever losing one or the other and it was always up to me to remember them for myself and for her and I had begun—

—DAA-DUM, da-da-da-da-da-dum, de-de-de, de-de-de, DAA-DUM, da-da-da-da-dum. Chopin. She played it all the time. It rattled the stuffed meerkat on the piano lid. Mother hated it. Play something pretty, Esme, she would say, not that dreadful—

—the word I definitely knew. Someone has been in and turned on the lights. The others are getting up and fiddling with the television switch and I would like to go back to my room but there is no one to help me just now so I will have to sit and wait and try to think of the word for the thing hanging from the ceiling. A structure of wire with material and a lightbulb inside, illuminated—

—may have told about the blazer. Did I? I forget. Esme. Is me. Esme. Wouldn't let go, they said. It's difficult to know whether—

—and when I first saw him I thought I might dissolve, like sugar in water. We were getting off the tram at Tollcross, it had broken down, the contact and the cabling had come apart, and I had been helping Mother with her messages so she and I were laden with boxes and parcels. We made it over to the pavement and there he was. Next to his mother. With boxes and parcels. We could have been mirror images. Mother and Mrs Dalziel discussed the weather and the tram and the health of their husbands, in that order, and Mrs Dalziel introduced her son. This is my James, she said, but of course I knew that already. The name Jamie Dalziel was familiar to every girl in Edinburgh. James, I said, and he took my hand in his. Very nice to meet you, Kitty, he replied, and I loved the way he said Kitty, the way he winked at me when Mother was looking down the road for the next tram, the way he carried the boxes as if they weighed nothing. That night I slid the glove I'd been wearing under my pillow. As we were leaving Mrs Dalziel said that I must come to their Hogmanay party. You and your sister, she said. She called him Jamie as they left. Jamie, mind the messages. It was only a week after that when I met him on the Meadows. He was with a friend, Duncan Lockhart, but I didn't look twice at him, of course. And where are you off to, he said, as he fell into step beside me, and I said, I'm waiting for my sister. I have a little sister too, he said and I said, oh, mine is not so little any more, she's taller than me, she'll be leaving school soon. And as I said this I saw her walking down the road. She came towards us and, you know, she barely even glanced at him. Hello, she said to me and I said, this is my sister, Esme, and he smiled that smile of his, took her hand and said, charmed. That was what he said: charmed. And she laughed, she actually laughed, and she pulled her hand away. Will you listen to yourself, she said to him, and added, eejit, just loud enough for him to hear. When I looked back at him I saw that he was looking at her, I saw the way it was, that he might dissolve like sugar in water, and when I saw this I—

—problem had also been that whenever we went anywhere, she and I, and we did get invitations quite regularly, due to the family name, of course, even though she had refused to make friends with any of the girls at her school. Harpies, she said they were, that was the word. But whenever we went somewhere, a tennis party or tea or a dance, she would always do something strange, something unexpected. Rattling away on the piano, talking to a dog for the entire time, once climbing a tree and sitting there in the branches, staring into space and twiddling at that wild hair of hers. There were some people, I am certain, who stopped inviting us. Because of her behaviour. And I have to say I felt that very keenly. Mother said I was right to. That you, she said, who never conducts herself in any manner other than one of the utmost decorum, should suffer because of her. It is not right. There was one time I over-heard—

—mine was white organdie with an orange-blossom trim and I didn't want the holly to tear it so she carried the wreath. She cared little for her dress. Scarlet velvet, she'd wanted. Crimson. But she got burgundy taffeta. And she said it didn't fit properly, the seams weren't straight and even I could see that but such things mattered so much to her that—

—a girl comes to crouch in front of me and I see that she is unlacing my shoes and taking them off and I say to her, I took it, I took it, and I've never told anyone. The girl looks up at me and she titters. You tell us every day, she says. I know she is lying so I say, it was my sister's, you know. And she just turns to speak to someone over her shoulder and—

—overheard someone saying something about her, laughing at her. A girl in a seersucker blouse, lovely it was, pintucks all down the front. She was pointing at Esme and nudging the two men with her. Look at the Oddbod, she said. The Oddbod, they called her. So I looked and would you believe it she was in an armchair and she had one leg slung over the arm, a book in her lap, her legs wide apart under her skirt. It was a dance, for heaven's sake. I had been so pleased to be asked, it was a good family, and I knew that after this we should never be asked again. I had to go over and my face was burning and every person in the room was watching me and I said her name twice and she was so engrossed in whatever it was she was reading she didn't hear me and so I had to shake her by the arm. And she looked up at me and it was as if she was waking from sleep. She stretched. She actually stretched and she said, hello, Kit. And then she must have seen that I was on the verge of tears because her face fell and she said, what is it? And I said, you. You are ruining my chances. And, you know, she said, chances of what? And I realised that if I were to successfully—

—the way he looked at her—

—the meerkat shaking in its glass box. My grandfather had caught it, apparently. Our grandmother was very fond of it. It had a very aggrieved expression, that was the word she used, aggrieved. And no wonder, she would say, looking up at it as she played, who would want to be shut up inside a—

—DAA-DUM, da-da-da-da-da-dum. I remember that—

And they walk, Esme and Iris, Esme behind the girl, Iris, looking at the backs of her heels in their red shoes, the way they disappear, reappear, disappear as she moves along the pavement in North Berwick. Iris has told her they are going back to the car now and Esme is looking forward to getting into it, to folding herself into the seat and perhaps the girl will put on the radio again and they will have music as they drive back.

She is thinking, as she walks, about that argument with her father, on an evening just before bed when the fire was dying down, and Kitty, her mother and the grandmother were busy with what they called their handwork and her mother had just asked her where was the tapestry square she'd given her. And Esme couldn't reply that she had hidden it, stuffed it down behind the chair cushions in her room.

'Put the book away, Esme,' her mother had said. 'You have read enough for tonight.'

But she couldn't because the people on the page and the room they were in were holding her fast but then her father was there in front of her and he snatched the book away, shut it without saving her page, and suddenly there was only the room she was in. 'Do as your mother asks,' he said, 'for God's sake.'

She'd sat up and the fury was within her, and instead of saying, please give me my book, she said, I want to stay on at school.

She hadn't meant to. She knew it wasn't the time to bring this up, that it would get nowhere, but it felt sore within her, this desire, and she couldn't help herself. The words came out from where they'd been hidden. Her hands felt strange and useless without the book and the need to stay at school had risen up and come out of her mouth without her knowing.

There was a silence in the room. Her grandmother glanced up at her son. Kitty glanced at their mother, then looked back at her work. What was it she was making again? Some ridiculous piece of lace and ribbonry for 'her trousseau', as she called it, with the affected French accent that made Esme want to scream. The maid had said recently, you'll be needing to find yourself a husband first, hen, and Kitty had been so upset she had run from the room, so Esme knew better than to criticise the growing heap of lace and silk in their cupboard.

'No,' her father had said.

'Please.' Esme stood. She clasped her hands together to keep them still. 'Miss Murray says I could get a scholarship and after that perhaps university and—'

'There would be no profit in it,' her father said, as he settled himself back into his armchair. 'My daughters will not work for a living.'

She had stamped her foot – crack – and it made her feel better, even though she knew it wouldn't help, that it would make everything worse.

'Why ever not?' she'd cried, because she had felt something closing about her of late. She couldn't bear the thought that in a few months she'd be here in this house with no reason to go from it, watched over by her mother and her grandmother all day. Kitty would go soon, taking her lace and ribbons with her. And there would be no escape, no relief from these walls, from this room, from this family until she married, and the thought of that was as bad, if not worse.

They are at the car. Iris unlocks it and Esme sees that an orange light flashes on its side. She opens the door and climbs in.

It had been only a day, maybe two, later when she and Kitty were sitting in their bedroom. Kitty was again sewing stitches into whatever it was – a nightdress, a slip, who knows? Esme had been at the window, watching her breath flatten and whiten on the glass, then dragging her fingers through it, hearing them screech against the pane.

Their grandmother swept into the room. 'Kitty,' there was an unaccustomed smile on her face, 'stir yourself. You have a visitor.'

Kitty put down her needle. 'Who?'

Their mother appeared behind the grandmother. 'Kitty,' she said, 'quickly, put that away. He's here, he's down-stairs—'

'Who is?' Kitty asked.

'The Dalziel boy. James. He has the newspaper but we mustn't be long.'

Esme watched from the window-seat as her mother started fiddling with Kitty's hair, tucking it behind her ears, then releasing it.

'I said I would come to fetch you,' Ishbel was saying, her voice cracking with delight, 'and he said, "Marvellous." Did you hear that? "Marvellous." So, quick, quick. You look very nice and we'll come with you, so you needn't—' Ishbel turned and, catching sight of Esme at the window, said, 'You too. Quickly now.'

Esme took the stairs slowly. She had no desire to meet one of Kitty's suitors. They all seemed the same to her – nervous men with over-combed hair, scrubbed hands and pressed shirts. They came and drank tea, and she and Kitty were expected to talk to them while their mother sat like an umpire in a chair across the room. The whole thing made Esme want to burst into honesty, to say, let's forget this charade, do you want to marry her or not?

She dawdled on the landing, looking at a grim, grey-skied watercolour of the Fife coast. But her grandmother appeared in the hall below. 'Esme!' she hissed, and Esme clattered down the rest of the stairs.

In the drawing room, she plumped down in a chair with high arms in the corner. She wound her ankles round its polished legs and eyed the suitor. The same as ever. Perhaps a little more good-looking than some of the others. Blond hair, an arrogant forehead, fastidious cuffs. He was asking Ishbel something about the roses in a bowl on the table. Esme had to repress the urge to roll her eyes. Kitty was sitting bolt upright on the sofa, pouring tea into a cup, a blush creeping up her neck.

Esme began playing the game she often played with herself at times like this, looking over the room and working out how she might get round it without touching the floor. She could climb from the sofa to the low table and, from there, to the fender stool. Along that and then—

She realised her mother was looking at her, saying some-thing.

'What was that?' Esme said.

'James was addressing you,' her mother said, and the slight flare of her nostrils meant, Esme knew, that she'd better behave or there would be trouble later.

'I was just saying,' the James person began, sitting forward in his chair, his elbows on his knees, and suddenly there was something familiar about him. Had Esme met him before? She wasn't sure, 'how beautiful your mother's garden is.'

There was a pause and Esme realised that it was her turn to speak. 'Oh,' she said. She couldn't think of anything else.

'Perhaps you would show me round it?'

From her chair, Esme blinked. 'Me?' she said.

Everyone was looking at her suddenly. Her mother, her grandmother, Kitty, James. And her mother's expression was so disconcerted, so appalled, that for a moment Esme thought she might laugh. Her grandmother's head was swiv-elling from James to Esme, then to Kitty, and back again to James. Some realisation was dawning there as well. She was swallowing rapidly and had to make a grab for her teacup.

'I can't,' Esme said.

James smiled at her. 'Why is that?'

'I . . .' Esme thought for a moment '. . . I've hurt my leg.'

'Have you?' James sat back in his chair and surveyed her, his eyes travelling over her ankles, her knees. 'I'm sorry to hear that. How did it happen?'

'I fell,' Esme mumbled, and pushed a piece of fruit cake between her teeth to signal that that was the end of the conversation and, luckily, her mother and grandmother came to her rescue, falling over themselves to offer him the company of her sister.

'Kitty would be happy to—'

'Why don't you go with Kitty, she's—'

'— show you some interesting plants in the far corner—'

'— terribly knowledgeable about the garden, she helps me quite often there, you know—'

James stood. 'Very well,' he said, and offered Kitty his arm. 'Shall we go, then?'

As they left, Esme uncurled her ankles from the chair legs and allowed herself to roll her eyes, just once, up to the ceiling and back. But she thought James caught her because she realised too late that, as he went out through the door with Kitty, he was looking back at her.

And Esme doesn't remember how many days passed before the time when she was making her way under the trees. It was early evening, she remembers that. She'd stayed late at school to finish an essay. Fog was sinking over the city, gluing itself to the houses, the streets, the lights, the black branches overhead, making them seem blurred and indistinct. Her hair was damp under her school beret and her feet icy inside her shoes.

She hefted her satchel to the other shoulder and, as she did so, was aware of a dark shape flitting through the trees on the Meadows. She tried not to glance back and increased her pace. The fog was thickening, grey and wet.

She was blowing on her frozen fingers when, from nowhere, a figure loomed up beside her in the gloom and seized her arm. She screamed and, grasping the leather strap of her satchel, belted the person round the head with all the combined weight of her books. The spectre grunted then swore, staggering backwards. Esme was off down the pavement before she heard him calling her name.

She stopped and waited, peering into the fog. The figure appeared again, materialising from the grey, this time with a hand held to his head.

'What did you want to go and do that for?' he was growling.

Esme stared at the man, puzzled. She couldn't believe that this was the horrid spectre from the gloom. He had fair hair, a smooth face, a good overcoat and a well-bred Grange accent. 'Do I know you?' she said.

He had flipped a handkerchief from a pocket and was dabbing at his temple. 'Look,' he was exclaiming, 'blood. You've drawn blood.' Esme glanced at the white cotton and saw three drops of scarlet. Then he suddenly seemed to hear what she had said. 'Do you know me?' he repeated, aghast. 'Don't you remember?'

She looked at him again. He summoned up a feeling of constriction in her, she noticed, of stillness and boredom.

Something clicked in her head and she remembered. James. The suitor who'd liked the garden.

'I came to your house,' he was saying. 'There was you, your sister Katy, and—'

'Kitty.'

'That's right. Kitty. It was only the other day. I can't believe you didn't recognise me.'

'The fog,' Esme said vaguely, wondering what he wanted, when she could decently walk off. Her feet were freezing.

'But I first met you over there.' He gestured behind him. 'Do you remember that?'

She nodded, suppressing a smile. 'Uh-huh. Mr Charming.'

He gave a mock bow, took her hand as if to kiss it. 'That's me.'

She pulled her hand away. 'Well. I must be going. Goodbye now.'

But he took her arm and looped it through his and set off with her down the pavement. 'Anyway,' he said, as if they were still talking, as if she hadn't just said goodbye, 'none of this is the point because the point is, of course, when are you coming to the pictures with me?'

'I'm not.'

'I can assure you,' he said, with a smile, 'that you are.'

Esme frowned. Her footsteps stuttered. She tried to wrest her fingers out from under his but he held them firm. 'Well, I can assure you that I'm not. And I should know.'

'Why?'

'Because it's up to me.'

'Is it?'

'Of course.'

'What if,' he said, applying heavier pressure to her hand, 'I were to ask your parents? What then?'

Esme snatched away her hand. 'You can't ask my parents if I'll go to the pictures with you.'

'Can't I?'

'No,' she said. 'And, anyway, even if they said yes I still wouldn't go. I'd rather . . .' she tried to think of something extreme, something to make him go away '. . . I'd rather stick pins in my eyes.' That ought to do it.

But he was grinning as if she'd said something extremely flattering. What was wrong with the man? He readjusted his glove and twitched his cuff, looking her up and down as if considering whether or not he should eat her.

'Pins, eh? They don't teach you many manners at that school of yours, do they? But I like a challenge. I shall ask you one more time. When are you going to come to the pictures with me?'

'Never,' she retorted. Again, she was amazed to see him smile. She didn't think she'd ever been as rude to anyone as she'd been to him.

He stepped up close to her and she made sure to hold her ground. 'You're not like other girls, are you?' he murmured.

Despite herself, she was interested in this declaration. 'Aren't I?'

'No. You're no drawing-room shrinking violet. I like that.

I like a bit of temper. Life's dull without it, don't you think?'
The white of his teeth gleamed in the dark and she could
feel his breath on her face. 'But seriously now,' he said and
his tone was firm, magisterial, and Esme thought this was
how he might speak to his horses. The thought made her
want to giggle. Wasn't the Dalziel family famous for its
equestrian accomplishments? 'I'm not going to waste any
pretty words and persuasive phrases on you. I know you
don't need them. I want to take you out, so when will it
be?'

'I already told you,' she said, holding his gaze. 'Never.'

She felt him catch her wrist and she was surprised by
the insistence, the power of his grip. 'Let go,' she said, stepping away from him. But he held on, fast. She struggled.
'Let go!' she said. 'Do you want me to hit you again?'

He released her. 'Wouldn't mind,' he drawled. As she
walked away, she heard him call after her: 'I'm going to
invite you to tea.'

'I won't come,' she threw back over her shoulder.

'You damn well will. I'm going to get my mother to invite
your mother. Then you'll have to come.'

'I won't!'

'We've got a piano you could play. A Steinway.'

Esme's steps slowed and she half turned. 'A Steinway?'

'Yes.'

'How did you know I played the piano?'

She heard him laugh, the noise bouncing along the wet
pavement towards her. 'I did a little research on you. It

wasn't difficult. You seem to be rather notorious. I found out all kinds of things. Can't say what, though. So, you'll come to tea?'

She turned towards home again. 'I doubt it.'

Iris is turning the car off the coast road and on to the bypass for Edinburgh, Esme in the seat next to her, when she decides that maybe she should call Luke. Just to check. Just to make sure he hasn't done anything stupid.

As they accelerate down the sliproad towards the bypass, she takes her phone out of her pocket with one hand, keeping her eyes on the road and her foot on the pedal. She had told Luke in the past that she would never call at the weekend. She knows the rules. But what if he has told her? He can't have. He won't have. Surely.

Iris sighs and flings the phone on to the dashboard. It may be time, she reflects, to excise Luke from her life.

Esme shifted in the armchair. It was covered with a heavy brown fabric, balding on the arms. The sharp ends of feathers poked through it, needling her thighs. She shifted again, making her mother glance at her. She had to stop herself sticking out her tongue. Why had she made her come?

They were having a conversation about the imminent party, the difficulty about invitations in Edinburgh, the best dairy from which to obtain fresh cream. Esme attempted to listen. Maybe she should say something. She hadn't spoken yet and she felt it might be time for her to open her mouth. Kitty, on the sofa with their mother, was managing to put in a few comments, though heaven only knew what she had to say about the purchase of cream. Mrs Dalziel made some remark about the cut on Jamie's face and how he'd walked into a low-growing branch in the fog. Esme froze, all possible conversational gambits dying in her throat.

'It looks terribly painful, James,' Esme's mother said.

'It isn't,' he said, 'I assure you. I've had worse.'

'I hope it's healed in time for your party. Would you be able to identify the tree? Someone should maybe tell the authorities. It sounds dangerous.'

Jamie cleared his throat. 'It is dangerous. I think I will alert the authorities. Good idea.'

Esme, her face hot, looked about for somewhere to put down her teacup. There was no convenient table or surface nearby. The floor? She peered over the arm of the chair at the parquet. It seemed an awful long way down and she wasn't sure if she could balance it on the saucer at the angle the drop required. Imagine shattering one of Mrs Dalziel's teacups. Kitty and their mother had placed theirs on a small table in front of them. Esme was getting desperate. She twisted round once more to see if there wasn't a table the other side of the enormous chair and suddenly Jamie was there, his hand outstretched. 'Will I take that for you?' he was saying.

Esme put the teacup into his hand. 'Oh,' she said, 'thank you.'

He winked at her as he took it and Esme saw that Mrs Dalziel was looking at them with a gaze sharp as a knife.

'Tell me, Mrs Lennox,' Mrs Dalziel said in a slightly raised voice, 'what plans do you have for Esme when she leaves school?'

'Well,' her mother began, and Esme felt a flush of indignation. Why not ask her directly? Did she not have a voice of her own?

She opened her mouth without the faintest idea of what was going to come out of it, until she heard: 'I am going to travel the world.' And she was rather pleased with this notion.

Jamie, from the chair opposite, snorted with laughter and had to smother it, coughing into a handkerchief. Kitty was regarding her, stunned, and Mrs Dalziel brought up a pair of spectacles, through which she took a long look at Esme, from her feet all the way up to a point above her head.

'Is that so?' Mrs Dalziel said. 'Well, that should keep you busy.'

Esme's mother replaced her teaspoon on a saucer with a clash. 'Esme is . . .' she began '. . . she is still so young . . . She has some rather . . . extreme views on . . .'

'So I see.' Mrs Dalziel shot a look at her son, who turned his head towards Esme and Esme saw, at the same moment, her sister. Kitty's eyes were cast down towards the floor but she lifted them to Jamie for a split second and then dropped

154

them again. Esme saw her change in that instant, red staining her neck, her lips pressing together. Esme sat motionless, in shock, then she sat forward and got to her feet.

All faces in the room turned towards her. Mrs Dalziel was frowning, reaching for her spectacles again. Esme stood in the middle of the carpet. 'Might I play your piano?' she said.

Mrs Dalziel put her head on one side, pressed two fingers to her mouth. She glanced again at her son. 'By all means,' she said, inclining her head.

Jamie leapt up. 'I'll show you where it is,' he said, and hustled Esme out into the corridor. 'She likes you,' he whispered, as he shut the door behind him.

'She does not. She thinks I'm the Devil incarnate.'

'Don't be ridiculous. She's my mother. I can tell. She likes you.' He put a hand round her arm. 'This way,' he said, and led her towards a room at the back of the house, with leaves pressed up against the windows, giving a peculiar greenish glow to the walls.

Esme seated herself on the stool and ran her hands over the black-wood lid, the gold letters that spelt out 'Steinway'.

'I don't see that it matters anyway,' she said, as she lifted the lid.

'It doesn't,' he said, leaning on the piano, 'you're right. I can have whomever I like.'

She shot him a look. He was gazing at her, lips curled in a smile, hair falling into his eyes, and she wondered for a moment what it would be like to be married to him. She tried to imagine herself in this big house with its dark walls, its windows crushed in by plants, its winding staircase and a room upstairs that would be hers and one that would be his, close by. She could have this, she saw with surprise. It could be hers. She could be Esme Dalziel.

She stretched her fingers into a soft chord. 'It doesn't matter,' she said, not looking at him, 'because I'm not going to get married. To anyone.'

He laughed. 'Are you not?' He moved round and seated himself next to her on the stool, right next to her. 'Let me tell you something,' he murmured, close to her ear, and Esme fixed her eyes on the rivet on the music stand, on the curling *y* of 'Steinway', on the knife-crease of his trouser leg. She had never been as close to a man as this before. His hand was pressing at her waist. He smelt of something sharp, some kind of cologne, and of fresh leather. It was not unpleasant. 'Of all the girls I've met, you seem the one most suited for marriage.'

Esme was taken aback by this. It was not at all what she had expected him to say. She turned to him. 'I do?' But his face was close to hers, blurringly close, and she was struck by the thought that he might try to kiss her so she turned her head back.

'Yes,' he whispered into her ear, 'you have the spirit for it. You could match a man, stroke for stroke. You wouldn't be cowed by it.'

'By marriage?'

'Most women are. You see it all the time. Pretty young

girls who become matronly bores the minute they get a ring on their finger. You wouldn't be like that. You wouldn't be changed at all. I can't imagine you being changed by anything. And that's what I want. That's why I want you.'

The hand on her waist tightened and she was drawn towards him and she felt him press his lips to her skin, at the place where her blouse ended and her neck began. The shock was electrifying. It was the most intimate thing anyone had ever done to her. She turned to look at him in amazement and he was laughing at her, his chest pressed to her shoulder, and she wanted to say: is it that, is that what it is, is that what it would be like, like that? But she heard the door to the parlour open and the voice of Jamie's mother could be heard: 'Why don't you go and join them, Kitty, dear?'

She pulled her gaze from Jamie just in time to see her sister step into the room. Kitty came through the door and raised her head. Esme saw her blink, very slowly, then look away. Esme put the flat of her hands to the wood of the piano stool and pushed herself into a standing position. She went to her sister's side and linked her arm through hers but Kitty kept her face averted and her arm felt heavy, lifeless.

In real time, Esme is in the car, being driven back from the sea to Edinburgh. She has decided to pretend to fall asleep. Not because she's tired. Because she needs to think. She lets her head fall back and she closes her eyes. After a few moments, the girl, Iris, leans over and turns off the radio. The orchestral music, which in truth Esme had been enjoying, is silenced.

This is the single nicest act Esme has witnessed in a long time. It almost makes her cry, which is something that never happens any more. She is overcome by an urge to open her eyes and take the girl's hand. But she doesn't. The girl is unsure of her, she wishes she weren't there – Esme knows this. But imagine. She was still worried about the radio music disturbing her sleep. Imagine that.

In order not to cry, she thinks. She concentrates.

On New Year's Eve afternoon, her mother and Kitty go out to the dressmaker, a small woman with a bun, to pick up the dresses. While they are out, Esme wanders into her mother's room. She peers into her jewellery box, she opens the pots on her dressing-table, she tries on a felt hat. She is sixteen.

She checks the street. Empty. She cocks her head and listens to the house. Empty. She twists her hair into a rope and pins it high on her head. She opens her mother's wardrobe. Tweed, fur, wool, tartan, cashmere. She knows what she is looking for. She has known since she came in here, since she heard the front door click shut. She has glimpsed it only a handful of times, at night, her mother gliding along the corridor between her father's room and hers. A négligé in aquamarine silk. She wants to know if the hem will swish round her ankles. She wants to know if the narrow straps will lie against her shoulders, just so. She wants to see the self she will be under all that sea-coloured lace. She is sixteen.

She feels it before she sees it – the cold caress of silk. It is right at the back, behind her mother's second-best suit. Esme slips it off its hanger, and it tries to escape her, slithering through her fingers to the floor. But she catches it round its waist and flings it to the bed. She pulls off her sweater, keeping her eyes on the pool of silk. She is about to dive in. Does she dare?

But she turns her head towards the car window. She opens her eyes. She does not want to think of this. She does not. Why should she? When the sun shines? When she is with the girl who cares if she sleeps well or not? When she is being driven along a road she doesn't recognise? The city she knows, the buildings, the line of roofs, but nothing else. Not the road, not the strings of orange lights, not the shopfronts. Why should she think of this?

—no small amount of shame in it, I can tell you. It has never happened in our family, ever. And for it to befall my own son. Times have changed, he said to me, and I said, you have to work at a marriage, God knows, your father and I did, thinking, if he only knew. But. Is it absolutely necessary to divorce, couldn't you— and he interrupted me. We're not married, he said, so technically it's not a divorce. Well. Of course I've kept that quiet in our circle. For the sake of the child. I never liked the wife or whatever she is. Shapeless clothes and unkempt hair. He says it is amicable. And I must say he is very good about keeping in touch with the child. A pretty little thing, she is, she has a look of my mother but in terms of character I think she reminds me most of—

—I do not know if I like yoghurt. A woman is asking me and I don't know the answer. What shall I say? I'll say no. She'll take it away and I won't need to think about it. But she hasn't waited for my answer, she has left it beside my plate. I'll pick it up and that long shiny thing she has left with it, silver it is, with a round head, the name of it is—

—he would always count them after a dinner party. Wrapping wet bundles of them in teacloths, polishing their ends and counting them back into the velvet-lined cutlery box. It used to drive me mad. I had to leave the room. I couldn't stand the sound of him murmuring the numbers under his breath, the way he stacked them into battalions of ten along the emptied table. Is there anything more likely to drive you completely out of your—

—pebbles. I taught her to count with pebbles I collected from the garden in India. I found ten beautiful, even, smooth pebbles that I lined up on the path for her. Look, I said, one, two, three, do you see? She had bare feet, her hair tied in a ribbon. Onetwofree, she said back to me, and smiled. No, I said, look, one, two, three. She caught them up, the pebbles, four in one hand and six in the other. Before I could stop her, she hurled them up into the air. As they rained back down I ducked. Miraculous, really, that she wasn't hit, if you think about—

—the mother brings the child to visit me. She and I don't have much to say to each other but I confess I have surprised myself by conceiving a fondness for the little girl. Grandma, she said to me the other day, and she was making these circles in the air with her arm, watching herself as she did it, when I do something my skeleton does it too. And I said, you are quite right, my dear. My son may have other children, who knows, he is still young. If he meets someone else, someone nice, someone more suitable. I would like that. It would be better for Iris not to be an only one and I should know because—

—and when I found them, when I came upon them sitting together like that, the pair of them on the piano stool, and him gazing at her as if he was seeing something rare and precious and desirable, I wanted to stamp my foot, to shout, do you know what they call her, they call her the Oddbod, people laugh about her behind her back, don't you know that? I knew that it could not be, that it must not happen, that I had to—

—I do not like yoghurt. It is cold, oversweet and there are hidden lumps of sloppy, slippery fruit. I do not like it. I let the spoon drop to the floor and the yoghurt makes an interesting fan-shape over the carpet and—

There is a loud, sudden crack, like thunder, and she is thrown backwards. She feels the cold of the mirror against the bare skin of her arm. Her face is ringing with heat, with pain, and Esme realises that her father has slapped her.

'Take it off!' he is shouting. 'Take it off this instant!'

Esme's fingers are made slow with shock. She fumbles at the neckline for the buttons but they are tiny, silk-faced, and her hands are trembling. Her father bears down on her and tries to pull the négligé over her head. Esme is plunged into an ocean of silk, suffocated by it, drowning in it. Her hair and the silk are in her mouth, gagging her, she cannot see, she loses her balance and stumbles into a hard corner of furniture, and all the time her father is shouting words, horrible words, words she has never heard before.

Suddenly her mother's voice cuts into the room. 'That's enough,' she says.

Esme hears her shoes across the floor. The silk noose is loosened from around her head, yanked down. Her mother stands before her. She doesn't look at her. She unbuttons the négligé and, in one movement, strips it off her, and Esme is reminded of a man she once saw skinning a rabbit.

She blinks and looks around her. Seconds ago, she was before the mirror, alone, the hem of the négligé in one hand, and she was turning sideways to see how it looked from the back. Now she is in her underwear, her hair pulled loose about her shoulders, her arms gripped round her. Kitty is by the door, still in her outdoor coat, her hands twisting at her gloves. Her father stands at the window, his back to them. No one speaks.

Her mother gives the négligé a shake, and takes a long time to fold it, lining up the seams and smoothing out creases. She places it on the bed.

'Kitty,' her mother says, without looking at anyone, 'would you please fetch your sister's dress?'

They listen to Kitty's footsteps recede down the corridor.

'Ishbel, she is not going to the party after this,' her father mutters. 'I really think—'

Her mother interrupts. 'She is. She most certainly is.'

'But what on earth for?' her father says, rooting for a handkerchief in his pocket. 'What is the point in sending a girl like that to such a gathering?'

'There is a rather great point.' The mother's voice is low and determined, and she takes Esme's arm and pulls her towards the dressing-table. 'Sit,' she commands, and pushes Esme on to the stool. 'We shall get her ready,' she says, picking up a hairbrush. 'We shall make her look pretty, we shall send her to the ball, and then,' she raises the hairbrush and brings it down in a vicious sweep through Esme's hair, 'we shall marry her off to the Dalziel boy.'

'Mother,' Esme begins tremulously, 'I don't want to—'

Her mother brings her face down to hers. 'What you want,' she murmurs, almost lovingly, into her ear, 'does not come into this. The boy wants you. Goodness knows why, but he does. Your kind of behaviour has never been tolerated in this house and it never will be. So, we shall see if a few months as James Dalziel's wife will be enough to break your spirit. Now, stand up and get yourself dressed. Here's your sister with your frock.'

Life can have odd confluences. Esme will not say serendipity: she loathes the word. But sometimes she thinks there must be something at work, some impulse, some collision of forces, some kinks in chronology.

Here she is, thinking about this, and she suddenly sees that the girl is driving the car past the very house. A coincidence? Or something else?

Esme twists in her seat to look at it. The stonework is dirty, stained dark in patches; a torn poster is pasted on the garden wall. Large brown plastic bins clog the path. The window paint is peeling and cracking.

They walked there, in their party shoes. Kitty was so in love with her dress she wouldn't carry the wreath of holly, so Esme carried it for her. Kitty held Esme's bag, which she had decorated with sequins for her. When they arrived and they were standing in the hallway, taking off their coats, Esme reached out to take the bag and Kitty let her have it: she uncurled her fingers and released it. But she didn't look at her. Maybe Esme should have known then, she should have seen the invisible weft and weave taking shape round her, should have heard the tightening of the strings. What if, she always thinks. She has spent her life half strangled by what-ifs. But what if she had known then, if a kink had occurred in the chronology and she'd seen what was about to happen? What would she have done? Turned round and gone home again?

It didn't and she didn't. She handed over her coat, she took her sequined bag from Kitty, she waited as her sister fiddled with her hair in the mirror, as she greeted a girl they knew. Then Kitty caught up with her and they went up the stairs, towards the lights, towards the music, towards the muffled roar of conversation.

Two girls at a dance, then. One seated, one standing. It was late, almost midnight. The younger girl's dress was too tight round her ribs. The seams strained, threatening separation, if she breathed in too deeply. She tried slumping her back in a curve, but it was no use: the dress bunched up like loose skin round her neck. It wouldn't behave, wouldn't act as if it was really hers. Wearing it was like being in a three-legged race with someone you didn't like.

She stood up to watch the dance. A complicated reel to which she didn't know the steps, the women getting passed from man to man, then returned to their partners. She turned to her sister. 'How long until midnight?'

Kitty was sitting on a chair next to her, a dance-card open on her lap. She had the pencil gripped between her gloved fingers, poised above the page. 'Another hour or so?' Kitty said, absorbed in reading the names. 'I'm not sure. Go and look at the clock in the hall.'

But Esme didn't go. She stood watching the reel until it spun to a standstill, until the music stopped, until the symmetrical formations of dancers broke down into a mêlée of people returning to their seats. When she saw the good-looking blond boy of the house making his way towards her, she quickly turned her back. But she was too late.

'May I have this dance?' he said, closing his fingers on hers.

She pulled them away. 'Why don't you ask my sister?' she whispered.

He frowned and said, loudly, too loudly so that Kitty heard, so that Esme saw Kitty hearing. 'Because I don't want to dance with your sister, I want to dance with you.'

She took her place opposite Jamie, in a set for Strip the Willow. They were the first couple, so as the music struck up, he came towards her, took her hands and whirled her about. She felt the stuff of her dress inflate, the room veer around her. The music beat thick and fast and Jamie took her hand and passed her along the row of men and whenever she came out of a spin, there he was, ready for her, his arm outstretched to take her. And at the last moment of their turn, when they had to join hands and dance to the end of the line, people clap-clapping them on their way, Jamie danced so fast and so far that they burst out of the room, on to the landing and it made Esme laugh and he whirled her round so that she felt dizzy and had to clutch his arm for balance and she was still laughing, and so was he, when he caught her to him, when he turned her more slowly, as if for a waltz, round and round under the chandelier, and she threw back her head to see the points of light kaleidoscoping above her.

Where does the hand become the wrist? Where does the shoulder become the neck? She will often think that this was the moment that tipped it, that if there was ever a point at which she could have changed things, this was it, when she was turning round and round beneath a chandelier on New Year's Eve.

He was propelling her in circles, still holding her tightly. She felt a wall brush against her back and this wall seemed to give way and they were overtaken by darkness, in some kind of small room, the music suddenly far away. Esme saw the looming shapes of furniture, heaps of coats, hats. Jamie had his arms round her and he was whispering her name. She could feel that he was about to kiss her, that one of his hands was touching her hair, and it occurred to her that she was curious to know what it was like, that a kiss from a man was something one ought to experience, that it could do no harm, either way, and as Jamie's face came down on hers, she waited, she held still.

It was a curious sensation. A mouth brushing hers, pressing hers, his arms tight round her. His lips were slippery and tasted vaguely meaty and she was struck by the ridiculousness of the situation. Two people in a cupboard, pressing their mouths together. Esme giggled; she turned her head away. But he was murmuring something in her ear. I beg your pardon, she said. Then he pressed her backwards, gradually, tenderly, and she felt herself topple, her feet losing their hold on the floor, and they landed on something soft and yielding, a pile of clothing of some sort. He was laughing softly and she was getting up and he was pulling her back and saying, you do love me, don't you, and they were both still smiling at this point, she thinks. But then it was different and she was really wanting to get up, she really thought she should, and he wouldn't let go. She was pushing at him, saying, Jamie, please, let's go back to the dance. His hands were on her neck, then, flailing with her skirts, on her legs.

She pushed at him again, this time with all her strength. She said, no. She said, stop. Then, when he grappled at the neckline of her dress, kneading at her breasts, fury flared in her and fear as well, and she kicked, she hit out at him. He jammed a hand over her mouth, said, wee bitch, in her ear and the pain of it, then, was so astonishing, she thought she was splitting, that he was burning her, tearing her in two. What was happening was unthinkable. She hadn't known it was possible. His hand over her mouth, his head ramming against her chin. Esme thought about how, perhaps, she would cut her hair after all, the sound of the rubber trees, how she must just keep breathing, a box she and Kitty kept under the bed with programmes of films, the number of sharps in F minor diminished.

And what seemed like a long time afterwards, they were on the landing again. Jamie was holding her wrist. He was leading her back towards the music. And, incredibly, the set for Strip the Willow was still going on. Did he think they were going to rejoin the dance? Esme looked at him. She looked at the candles, melting in pools of themselves, at the people circling and jumping in the dance, their faces tight with concentration, with pleasure.

She wrenched his hand off her wrist. It hurt her skin to

do it but she was free. She stretched her fingers into the air. She took two, three steps towards the doorway and there she had to stop. She had to lean her forehead against the wood. The edges of her vision wavered, like the line of a horizon in heat. A face swam up to hers and said something but the music was thick in her ears. The person took hold of her arm, gave her a shake, twitched her dress straight. It was, she saw, Mrs Dalziel. Esme parted her lips to say that she would like to see her sister, please, but what came out was a high-pitched noise that she couldn't stop, that she had no power over.

Then Esme was in the back of a car with Mrs Dalziel driving, and then they were home and Mrs Dalziel was telling her mother that Esme had had a wee bit too much to drink, made a fool of herself, and that she might feel better in the morning.

In the morning, though, Esme did not feel better. She did not feel better at all. When her mother came in through the door and said, exactly what happened last night, young lady, Esme sat up in bed and the noise came again. She opened her mouth and she screamed, she screamed, she screamed.

Iris lets Esme go ahead of her on the stairs and she notices how slowly she climbs, resting her weight on the banisters with every step. Maybe the outing was a bit much for her.

As they make the last turn, Iris stops. Along the bottom

of the door, she can see a line of glowing light. Someone is in her flat.

She pushes past Esme and, hesitating for just a moment, she turns the handle. 'Hello?' she calls into her hallway. 'Is anyone there?'

The dog brushes against her side. Iris curls her hand round his collar. She feels him stiffen. Then he raises his head and lets out a deep bark.

'Hello?' she says again, and her voice gives way in the middle of the word. A person appears in the kitchen doorway. A man.

'Don't you keep any food in this place?' Alex says.

She drops the dog's collar, darts towards her brother but stops just in front of him. 'You scared me,' she says, cuffing him on the arm.

'Sorry.' He grins. 'I thought I should come, seeing as—' He stops and looks over her shoulder.

Iris turns, she walks towards Esme. 'This is my brother,' she says.

Esme frowns. 'You have a brother?'

'A step-brother,' Alex says, stepping forward. 'She always forgets the "step". You must be Euphemia.'

Iris and Esme inhale in unison: 'Esme,' they say.

—and when she wouldn't stop—

—it was difficult as the whole family is full of only ones. I had no cousins and the man I was marrying was an only one too so there were no sisters-in-law-to-be. I needed someone to hold my flowers, to help me with my train, even though it was a modest size, to be with me in the moments just before the ceremony. You can't get married without a bridesmaid, Mother said, you'll have to think of someone. There were a couple of friends I could have asked but it seemed so odd after—

—and when she wouldn't stop screaming, Mother sent me out of the room and—

—it was only a fortnight later that Duncan Lockhart came to call. Nobody had been near us. No first-footers, no telephone calls. Nothing. The house was deathly quiet without her. Hours could pass without a single sound. In an odd way, we no longer seemed like a family, just a collection of people living in different rooms. Duncan came to see my father, ostensibly, but I'd met him at the party: we'd danced together. The Dashing White Sergeant, as I recall. He'd had very dry hands. And he mentioned seeing me that time on the Meadows. I, of course, had forgotten that he was even there. On the day he came, a cold January afternoon, I'd woken up and found ice on the insides of the windows. And I'd shut my eyes again because the room was still full of her things, her clothes, her books. Mother hadn't yet got round to—

—remember walking the floor with the baby in the middle of the night. I knew nothing about babies – you don't with your first, of course, so you fall back on your instincts. Keep moving, mine were telling me. He wouldn't eat, tiny wee

thing that he was, he would beat the air with his red fists.
I had to feed him with a muslin rag, soaked in milk. The
fourth day he took it, sucked at it, tentative at first, then
ravenous. And then we had pans of water on the stove,
boiling the bottles, at all times of day, nappies hung by the
fire, the air opaque with steam—

—and when she wouldn't stop screaming, Mother called
the doctor. I was told to leave the room but I listened
outside, my ear against the cold brass of the keyhole. I
could only hear when the doctor spoke to Esme – he seemed
to speak louder when addressing her, as if she was hard of
hearing or simple. He and Mother whispered to each other
for several minutes and then he raised his voice and said to
Esme, we are going to take you somewhere for a wee rest,
how would you like that? And she, of course, in her way
said she wouldn't like it at all, and then his voice went stern
and he said, we are not giving you a choice so—

—in the end, I asked a second cousin of Duncan's, a girl
I'd only met twice. She was younger than me and seemed
pleased. At least, my grandmother said grimly, we needn't
worry that she's going to outshine the bride. I took her to
Mrs Mac for the fitting. I didn't stay while she had it done,
I couldn't—

—did I tell about the blazer? I did. I think I did. Only
because they asked me, straight out. And I always make a
point of being as honest as I can. Did I tell about Canty
Bay as well? But what difference could it have made, really?
I always make a point of being as honest as I can. I was just

so eaten up, at that time. I never meant her to go for ever, just for as long as it took me to—

—so I was sent out of the room and I went, of course, but really I stayed behind the door and listened, and Mother was whispering with the doctor and I could barely hear a thing and I was worried in case my grandmother came up the stairs and caught me. Eavesdropping was very bad form, I knew that. I could barely hear, as I said, but Mother was saying something about how she was sick to her back teeth of these fits of shouting and raging. And the doctor rumbled something about hysteria and young girls, which offended me slightly as I have never behaved in such a fashion. He said the words *treatment* and *place* and *learn to behave*. And when I heard that I thought it sounded like a good idea, like a good plan for her because she had always been so—

—surprised me more than anything, how much you love them. You know you are going to and then the feeling itself, when you finally see them, when you hold their tiny body, is like a balloon that just goes on filling with air. Duncan's mother insisted we hire a nurse, a fearsome creature with feeding schedules and a starched apron, and I found my days were rather empty then. I missed Robert. I would go up to see him in the nursery, but before I got to the cot, the nurse would have got there first. We're asleep, she'd say, which always made me want to say, all of us? But I never did, of course. My mother-in-law said the nurse was worth her weight in gold and that we should be careful not to lose her. I wasn't sure, then, what it was I was supposed to be doing. The cook and the housekeeper ran the house, Duncan was at the office with my father, and Robert was with his nurse. Sometimes I would wander the house in the middle of the day, thinking that perhaps I ought to—

—dementia praecox is what they said for her. Father told me that when I asked him once. I made him write it down for me. Such pretty words, in a way, much prettier than they had any right to be. Of course no one uses them any more. I read that somewhere in an article. 'Outmoded term', is what it said. Today, the article told me, they would say 'schizophrenia', an ugly, horrible word, but a very grand one all the same, especially for something that is, after all—

—dress she made for the bridesmaid was actually better than anything she had ever made for me. I was in Mother's dress, of course, it had been specially fitted and let out for me. Many people remarked upon it. But the bridesmaid's dress had sequins, sewn into chiffon, all over—

—never meant her to go for ever, I never meant that at all. It was just that—

—she fought and kicked; my father had to help the doctor and together they managed it but right at the bottom of the stairs she got her hands round the banister. She clung on and the name she kept screaming was mine. I had my hands over my ears and my grandmother put her hands over mine but I could still hear her. KITTY! KITTY! KITTY! KITTY! I find I can still hear it now. I found a shoe later: it must have come off during the struggle in the hall because it was wedged under the hatstand and I took it and I sat down and leant my head into the banisters and—

—I watched through the banisters as my father shook his hand in the hallway. My father led the way into his study, and when he turned his back, Duncan did this gesture that later I would learn he always did when he was nervous. He put one hand up and over his head and smoothed down the hair on the other side. It looked so odd, it made me smile. I saw him glance at the shut doors around him, at the corridor reaching back into the house, and I did think, is he looking for me? But I would never have—

Her father doesn't speak in the car. She says his name, she says, Father, she touches his shoulder, she wipes her face, she tries to say, please. But he looks straight out of the windscreen, the doctor beside him. He doesn't speak as he gets out, as he and the doctor wedge her between them and walk her across the gravel and up the steps to a big building, high on a hill.

Inside the doors there is a heavy silence. The floor is tiles of marble, black white black white black white. Her father and the doctor shuffle and fumble with papers. They don't remove their hats. And then a woman she has never seen before, a woman dressed as a nurse, takes her arm.

'Father!' she shouts then. 'Father, please!' She yanks her arm away from the nurse, who lets out a small *tsk* noise from between her teeth. Esme sees her father stoop briefly over the drinking fountain, wipe his mouth with his handkerchief, then walk away over the chess squares of marble towards the door. 'Don't leave me here!' she cries out. 'Please! Please don't. I'll be good, I promise.'

Before the nurse takes her arm again, before another nurse materialises to take the other, before they have to pick her up and carry her away, Esme sees her father through the glass of the doors. He descends the steps, he buttons his coat, he puts on his hat, he glances up towards the sky, as if checking for rain, and then he disappears.

She is dragged backwards down a flight of stairs, along a corridor, a nurse on either side of her, their crooked arms linked through hers, her heels scraping along the floor. They have her in such a grip that she cannot move. The hospital appears to her as if on a reel of reversed film. They pass through some doors and she sees a high ceiling, a string of lights, rows of beds, the shapes of bodies hunched under the blankets. She hears coughs, moans, a person somewhere muttering to themselves. The nurses haul her on to a bed and they are puffing with the effort. Esme turns to look out of the window and sees bars, running up, running down.

Oh God, she says into the fetid air. She drives a hand into her head. Oh God. The shock of it all boils over into tears again. This cannot be, it cannot be. She reaches out and rips down the curtain, she kicks over the cabinet, she shouts, there has been a mistake, this is all a mistake, please listen to me. Nurses come running with wide leather belts and strap her to the bed, then walk away shaking their heads, straightening their caps.

She is left under the leather belts for a day and two nights. Someone comes and takes away her clothes. A woman with big silver scissors comes in the dusk and slices through her hair. This makes Esme wail and then weep, her tears sliding sideways down her face and into the pillow. She watches as the woman walks away with her hair held in one hand, like a whip.

There is a smell of disinfectant and floor polish and the person in the bed in the corner mutters all night long. A light in the ceiling flickers and buzzes. Esme cries. She struggles against the belts, tightly buckled, she tries to wriggle her way out, she shouts, please, please help me, until her voice is hoarse. She bites a nurse who tries to give her some water.

She finds herself haunted by the life she has left, been pulled out of. As light drains from the room at dusk, she thinks about how her grandmother will be descending the flagged steps into the kitchen to see how the dinner preparations are coming along, how her mother will be taking tea in the front parlour, counting out sugar lumps with clawed tongs, how the girls at school will be catching trams to their homes. It is inconceivable that she is not taking part in these events. How can they happen without her?

In the blue light of the second morning, a figure appears at her bed. It is indistinct, blurred, dressed in white. Esme stares up at it. There has been a stray hair across her eyes for hours now and she can't reach up to brush it away.

'Don't fuss and fight, girlie,' the figure whispers. Esme cannot see the face because of the shadows, because of the hair in her eye. 'You don't want to end up in Ward Four.'

'But there's been a mistake,' Esme croaks. 'I shouldn't be here, I don't—'

'You must be careful,' the woman says. 'Don't slide down a snake. The way you're carrying on—'

There is the sound of feet striking the floor and the nurse who cut Esme's hair appears. 'You!' she cries. 'Get back to your bed this instant.'

The figure flits away down the ward, vanishes.

Iris breaks an eggshell on the side of a bowl and watches the yolk drop. Alex leans against the fridge, tossing grapes into his mouth.

'So,' he says, and Iris feels a prickling irritation because she knows what he is about to say, 'what's been happening with you, then? Are you still seeing that guy?'

'What guy?' she says to the ceiling.

'You know who I mean,' Alex says affably. 'The lawyer guy.'

Iris fits one eggshell inside another. She is so grateful to him for not saying 'the married guy' that she has a burst of honesty. 'Yes,' she says, and wipes her hands on a tea-towel.

'Stupid,' he mutters.

She turns on him. 'Well, what about you?'

'What about me?'

'Aren't you still married to someone you decided you should never have married in the first place?'

He shrugs. 'I guess so.'

'Stupid yourself,' she retorts.

There is a short silence. Iris takes a fork and beats the eggs against the side of the bowl until they start to blend and froth. Alex pulls back a chair and sits at the table. 'Let's not fall out,' he says. 'You live your life, I live mine.'

Iris grinds pepper into the eggs. 'Fine.'

'So, what's happening with you and Mr Lawyer?'

She shakes her head. 'I don't know.'

'You don't know?'

'No. I do know. I just don't want to talk about it.' She tosses her hair out of her eyes and regards her brother, sitting at the kitchen table. He looks back at her for a long moment and then they smile at each other.

'I still don't know what you're doing here,' Iris says. 'Do you want dinner, by the way, or are you heading off?'

'You don't know what I'm doing here?' he repeats. 'Are you crazy? Or amnesiac? I get a phone call from you yesterday, saying you're in the clutches of a lunatic, so what do I do? Do I spend the weekend lounging around at home or do I come over here to save you from the madwoman? I didn't realise that the two of you would be off gallivanting at the seaside.'

Iris puts down the fork. 'Are you serious?' she says quietly. 'You came for me?'

Alex uncrosses and recrosses his legs. 'Of course I came for you,' he says, embarrassed. 'What else would I be doing here?'

Iris goes over to him, kneels and puts her arms round him. She feels the slightness of his torso, the smooth nap of his T-shirt. After a moment, he slings an arm round her shoulders, rocks her back and forth, and she knows they are both thinking about a time that neither of them wishes to return to. She gives him a small squeeze and smiles into his chest.

'You cut your hair,' he says, tugging at it.

'Yeah. You like it?'

'No.'

They laugh. Iris pulls away, and as she does so, Alex nods towards the spare room. 'She doesn't seem that mad,' he says.

'You know,' Iris puts her hands on her hips, 'I'm not sure she is.'

Alex is instantly wary. 'But she has been in a nuthouse for . . . How long was it again?'

'Doesn't necessarily mean she's mad.'

'Er, I think it probably does.'

'Why?'

'Hang on, hang on.' Alex holds up his hands, as if calming an animal. 'What are we talking about here?'

'We're talking,' she is suddenly impassioned, 'about a

sixteen-year-old girl locked up for nothing more than trying on some clothes, we're talking about a woman imprisoned for her whole life and now she's been given a reprieve and . . . and it's up to me to try to . . . I don't know.'

Alex stares at her for a moment, arms folded. 'Oh, God,' he says.

'What? What do you mean, "Oh, God"?'

'You getting on one of your things about this, aren't you?'

'One of my things?'

'One of your high horses.'

'I don't know what you mean,' Iris cries. 'I think it's out of order to—'

'She's not one of your rare vintage finds, you know.' He scratches invisible inverted commas in the air with his fingers.

For a moment, she is speechless. Then she snatches up the bowl of eggs. 'I don't know what you mean by that,' she snaps, 'but you can go to hell.'

'Look,' Alex says, more gently, 'just tell me—' He breaks off with a sigh. 'Just tell me you're not going to do anything stupid.'

'Like what?'

'Like . . . I mean, you are going to put her away, aren't you, find somewhere for her? Aren't you?'

She slams a frying-pan down on to the hob and slops oil into it.

'Iris?' Alex says, behind her. 'Tell me you're going to find somewhere to put her.'

She turns, pan in hand. 'You know, if you think about it, this flat really belongs to her.'

Alex buries his head in his hands. 'Oh, Christ,' he says.

Through the wall, Esme hears their voices. Or, rather, she hears the buzz, like bees in a jam-jar. The girl's voice is undulating, scaling peaks, then sliding down again, the boy's a near monotone. They might be arguing. The girl, Iris, makes it sound as if it's an argument but if it is it's very one-sided.

Her brother, she'd said. When Esme first saw him there, standing in the doorway, she wondered for a moment if he might be the lover. But then she looked back at Iris and saw that he wasn't. Not a proper brother, though, not a real one. A kind of half-attached one.

Esme bends her legs so that her knees break the surface of the bathwater, like islands in a lagoon. She has run the bath so hot that her skin is pinked, livid. Stay in as long as you like, Iris said to her, so she is. Steam has swarmed up the walls, the mirror, the inside of the window, the sides of the bottles on the shelf. Esme has no memory of this room. What would it have been in her day? The other rooms she can transpose, pull a photographic plate down over them, see them as they were: her room as the maid's bedroom, the sitting room as a place under the eaves where summer clothes were stored in cedarwood chests. Iris's bedroom used to be filled along one wall with glass jars for preserves. But for this room, she has no recall. The whole space she remembers as terribly dim and low-ceilinged when in fact the rooms are high enough, and airy. Just goes to show how fallible memory is.

She takes the soap from its dish and rubs it between her hands, like Aladdin with his lamp. A delicious sweet scent rises from it and she brings it up to her face and inhales. She wonders what the pair next door would say if she told them that this was her first unsupervised bath for over sixty years. She eyes the razor on the bath edge and smiles. The girl has left it there so casually. Esme has forgotten what it is like to be among unsuspicious people. She picks it up and touches the tip of her finger to its cool edge, and as she does so, it suddenly comes to her what used to be in this room.

Baby things. A wooden cot, with ribs like an animal skeleton. A high-chair with a string of coloured beads tied to the tray. And boxes full of tiny nightgowns, bonnets, booties, the sharp stink of mothballs.

Who would have been the last baby in this house? For whom were those jackets knitted, those gowns stitched? Who strung the beads on the high-chair? Her grandmother for her father, she would guess, but she cannot imagine it. The thought makes her want to giggle. Then she takes a breath, holds it and sinks under the water, letting her hair float around her like weeds.

She lay under the restraints. She watched a fly crawl with inching progress up the sickly green wall. She counted the number of noises she could hear: the drone of a car outside, the chatter of starlings, the wind tugging at a sash window, the mumble-mumble of the woman in the corner, the squeal of wheels from the corridor, the rustle of bedclothes, the sighs and grunts of the other women. She accepted spoonfuls of glutinous, tepid porridge from a nurse, swallowed them, even though her stomach rebelled, seemed to close at every mouthful.

In the middle of the morning, two women got into an argument.

'It's mine.'

'It never is.'

'It's mine. Give us it.'

'Get off it, it's mine.'

Esme raised her head to see them, pulling and yanking at something. Then the taller one, with greying hair scraped back into a messy bun, reached out and smacked the other's cheek. She immediately yelped, let go of whatever it was they were fighting over, then reared up, like an animal on its hind legs, and hurled herself at the other woman. Over they went, on to the floor, a strange eight-limbed creature, tussling and screaming, overturning a table, a basket of clothes. Nurses appeared from nowhere, shouting, calling to each other, blowing whistles.

'Stop that!' the ward sister shouted. 'Stop it at once.'

The nurses dragged them apart. The grey-haired woman went limp, sat down meekly on the bed. The other still fought, screaming, yelling, clawing at the ward sister's face.

Her gown rode up and Esme saw her buttocks, pale and round as mushrooms, the folds of her stomach. The ward sister caught her wrist, twisted it until the woman cried out.

'I'll put you in straits,' the nurse threatened. 'I will. You know I will.'

Esme saw the woman think about this and, for a moment, it seemed as though she would be calm. But then she bucked like a horse, kicking out, catching the ward sister on the knee, screaming a string of obscenities. The sister gave a short puff of breath and then, at some signal, the nurses bundled the woman off, down the ward, through a door and Esme listened as the noise grew fainter and fainter.

'Ward Four,' she heard someone whisper. 'She'll be taken to Ward Four.' And Esme turned her head to see who was speaking, but everyone was sitting on the beds, bolt upright, heads bowed.

When they unbuckled the belts, Esme kept very still. She sat on the bed, her hands tucked beneath her. She thought of animals that can be motionless for hours, crouched, waiting. She thought of the party game where you have to pretend to be a dead lion.

An orderly came round and dumped cloths and tubs of yellow, bitter-smelling polish on each bed. Esme slid off hers and stood, unsure, as the other women bent down to their knees as if about to pray, then began rubbing the polish into the floor, working backwards towards the door. Her legs felt stiff and immovable after the belts. She was just reaching for the cloth and polish on her bed when she saw one of the nurses point at her. 'Look at Madam,' she sniggered.

'Euphemia!' Sister Stewart yelled. 'Get down on your knees.'

Esme jumped at the shout. For a moment, she wondered why everyone was staring at her. Then she realised the sister meant her. 'Actually,' she began, 'I'm called—'

'Get down on your knees and get to work!' Sister Stewart bawled. 'You're no better than anybody else, you know.'

Esme knelt, shaking, wrapped the cloth round her fist and began rubbing at the floor.

Later, the other women came to speak to her. There was Maudie, who married Donald and then Archibald when she was still married to Hector, even though the one she really loved was Frankie, who was killed in Flanders. In her good moments, she would regale everyone with stories of her wedding ceremonies; in her bad ones, Maudie skipped up and down the ward with a petticoat tied under her chin, until Sister Stewart pulled it off and told Maudie to sit down and be a good girl or else. In the next beds were Elizabeth, who had seen her child crushed by a cart, and Dorothy, who was occasionally moved to strip off all her clothes. At the far end was an old woman the nurses called Agnes but who always corrected them by saying, 'Mrs Dalgleish, if you please.' She, Maudie told Esme, wasn't able to have children and sometimes she and Elizabeth got into arguments.

After a lunch of indeterminate grey soup, a Dr Naysmith

appeared. He walked between their beds, Sister Stewart two steps behind him, nodding at them in turn, occasionally saying, 'How are you feeling today?' The women, Elizabeth especially, got very excited, either launching into garbled monologues or bursting into tears. Two were taken off for a cold bath.

He stopped at Esme's bed, glanced at the name-tag on the wall beside her. Esme sat up, passed her tongue over her lips. She was going to tell him – she was going to tell him there had been a mistake, that she shouldn't be here. But Sister Stewart stood on tiptoe and whispered something into his ear.

'Very good,' he said, and moved on.

—and when he asked me, and here's me saying ask when what he said in the event was, I'd consider it a first-rate idea if we were wed. He said this on Lothian Road as we stood on the pavement. We had been to the pictures and I had waited and waited for him to take my hand. I'd dangled it over the arm of the seat, I'd removed my gloves, but he didn't seem to notice. I suppose I should have taken this as a—

—an hourglass with red sand, kept on top of the—

—and sometimes I take the little girl to the pictures. She is very grave. She sits with her hands laced in her lap, a slight frown on her face, attentive as the dwarfs go down into the mine, one by one, their little sticks over their backs.

Someone made it by putting drawings together very fast, she said to me last time, and I said, yes, and she said, who, and I said, a clever man, darling, and she said, how do you know it was a man? It made me laugh because, of course, I didn't know but somehow you do—

—watching the red sand falling through grain by grain and she said, does that mean the gap is exactly one grain wide? And I had no idea. I'd never thought of it like that. Mother said—

—the boy with them, I will never know. The changeling, I call him, but only to myself and the maid. The woman said to me, it would be lovely if you could be his grandma too. Well. There is no way on God's earth I would consider him any relation to me. A sullen, sulking child with mistrustful eyes. He is not of my blood. The little girl is very fond of him, though, and he has had a difficult life, by all accounts. A mother who upped and left, and how any woman can do that is beyond me. It goes against nature. The girl holds his hand, even though he is a year maybe two older than her, and he never leaves her side. I always want to pull her away from him, from his clammy boy clutches but of course you have to be the adult in these—

—a terrible thing, to want a—

—on Lothian Road, I snapped the clasp of my bag shut. I wanted to close my eyes for a moment. The lights of the carriages and trams were very tiring, especially after the picture we had just seen. He stood waiting and I looked at him and I saw the way his collar was pinched too tight, the way there was a dropped stitch in the scarf he was wearing and I wondered who knitted it for him, who loved him that much. His mother, at a guess, but I wanted to ask him. I wanted to know who loved him. I said yes, of course. I breathed it out, the way you are supposed to, I smiled shyly as I said it, as if it was all perfect, as if he'd gone down on his knee with roses in one hand and a diamond in the other. I couldn't bear any more nights in that room without—

—had gone away, everybody said. To Paris, one girl told me. To South America, another said. There was a rumour that Mrs Dalziel had sent him away to his uncle's house in England. And even though I rarely saw him anyway, the idea that I might not run into him, that the streets of the city did not contain him was enough to—

—and I found a clutch of letters, nesting in the bottom of a hat-box. This was perhaps months later. I was married by this time and I was looking for a hat to wear to a christening. Mother and Father had said one night, just before my wedding, that her name would not be mentioned again and that they would thank me if I would act accordingly. And I did, act accordingly, that is, although I thought about her a great deal more than they realised. So I pulled out the letters and—

—never meant it to be for ever. I would like to make that perfectly clear. I just meant for a while. I came into the parlour when my mother called for me and the doctor was there. She was upstairs, still shouting and carrying on. And they were whispering together and I caught the word 'away'. Kitty knows her best, my mother said, and the doctor from the hospital looked at me and he said, is there anything about your sister that concerns you? Anything she has confided in you that you think you should tell us? And I thought, I thought, and then I raised my head and I made my face a little sad, a little uncertain, and I said, well, she does think she saw herself once on the beach, when she was standing in the sea. And I could tell by the look on the doctor's face that I had done well, that I had—

—the way it snapped shut, that bag. I liked that. I always carried it half-way up my wrist, never too—

Iris carries the salad to the table and places it half-way between Esme and Alex. The salad servers she angles towards Esme. She allows herself a small, private smile at the idea that it would be almost impossible to find two more different dining companions.

'Where do you live?' Esme is saying.

'In Stockbridge,' Alex says. 'Before that, I lived in New York.'

'In the United States of America?' Esme asks, leaning forward over her plate.

Alex smiles. 'Absolutely correct.'

'How did you get there?'

'On a plane.'

'A plane,' she repeats, and she seems to consider the word. Then: 'I have seen planes.'

Alex leans over and chinks his glass against hers. 'You know, you're nothing like your sister.'

Esme, who is examining the salad in its bowl, turning it one way then the other, stops. 'You know my sister?'

Alex see-saws his hand in the air. 'I wouldn't go so far as to say I know her. I've met her. Many times. She didn't like me.'

'That's not true,' Iris protests. 'She just never—'

He leans conspiratorially towards Esme. 'She didn't. When my father and Sadie, Iris's mother, were together, Sadie thought it would be a good idea for me to come along on Iris's visits to her grandmother. God knows why. Her grandmother obviously wondered what I was doing there. She thought I was the cuckoo in the nest. She didn't like me fraternising with her precious granddaughter. Mind you, there wasn't an awful lot of love lost between her and Sadie, either, if you ask me.'

Esme takes a long look at Alex. 'Well, I like you,' she says finally. 'I think you're funny.'

'When did you last see her, anyway?'

'Who?'

'Your sister.' Alex is busy mopping his plate with a hunk of bread so it is only Iris who sees the look on Esme's face.

'Sixty-one years,' she says, 'five months and six days.'

Alex's hand with the bread is halted half-way to his mouth. 'You mean—'

'She never came to visit you?' Iris says.

Esme shakes her head, staring at her plate. 'I did see her once, a while after I went in, but . . .'

'But what?' Alex prompts, and Iris wants to shush him but also wants to hear the answer.

'We didn't speak . . .' Esme says, and her voice is level, she sounds like an actress going over her lines '. . . on that occasion. I was in a different room. Behind a door. She didn't come in.'

Alex looks over at Iris and Iris looks mutely back. He reaches for his wine glass, then seems to change his mind. He rests his hand on the table, then scratches his head. 'See?' he mutters. 'I always told you she was a bitch.'

'Alex,' Iris says, 'please.' She stands, lifting the plates from the table.

Esme sits at a table in the dayroom, feet curled round the chair legs. She mustn't cry, she mustn't cry. Never cry in public here. They'll threaten you with treatment or give you injections that make you sleep and wake up confused, disjointed.

She clenches her hands together to hold back the tears and looks down at the piece of paper in front of her. *Dear Kitty*, she has written. Behind her, Agnes and Elizabeth are sniping at each other.

'Well, at least I had a child. Some women never—'

'At least I didn't murder my child through neglect.

Imagine letting your own flesh and blood wander under a cart.'

To shut out their voices, Esme picks up her pencil. *Please come*, she puts. *Visitors are allowed on Wednesdays. Please*, she writes again, *please please*. She leans her forehead on her hand. Why does she never come? Esme doesn't believe that the nurses post her letters. Why else would she not come? What other explanation can there be? You are not well, the nurses tell her. You are not well, the doctor says. And Esme thinks she may be starting to believe this. There is a tremulousness to her suddenly. She can cry at nothing, at Maudie pinching her arm, at Dorothy stealing her afternoon biscuit. There are moments when she looks through the windows at the drop to the ground and thinks about the relief of the fall, the coolness of the air. And there is a soreness to her body, it aches, her head feels softened, muzzy. She has acquired a disturbingly acute sense of smell. The odour of print from a magazine someone is reading across a room can oppress her. She knows what will be on their plates at lunch just from sniffing the air. She can walk down the middle of the ward and can tell who has bathed this week and who has not.

She stands, to try to clear her head, to try to put some space between her and the rest of them, and walks to the window. Outside, it is a still day. Oddly still. Not a single leaf moves on a tree and the flowers in the beds all stand up straight, motionless. And she sees that on the lawn the patients from Ward Four are having their exercise. Esme touches her brow to the pane, watching them. They are in gowns, pale gowns, and they are drifting about like clouds. It's hard to tell if they are men or women as the gowns are loose and their hair is cut short. Some of them stand still, gazing ahead. One sobs into cupped hands. Another keeps giving a sharp, hoarse cry, which peters out in a mumble.

She turns away and looks round the dayroom. At least they wear their own clothes, at least they brush their hair every morning. She is not ill. She knows she is not ill. She wants to run, she wants to burst through the doors out into the corridor, to sprint along it and never come back. She wants to scream, let me out, how dare you keep me here. She wants to break something, the window, that framed picture of cattle in the snow, anything. And although she wants all this, and more, Esme makes herself sit at the table again. She makes herself walk across the room, bend her legs and sit in a chair. Like a normal person. The effort of it leaves a tremble in her limbs. She breathes deeply, presses her hands to the tabletop in case anyone is looking. She has to get out of here, she has to make them let her go. She pretends to be reading through what she has written.

And later, during her long-awaited appointment with the doctor, she tells him she is feeling better. Those are the words she has decided she must use. She must let them know that she, too, thinks she has been ill; she must acknowledge that they were right, after all. There had been something wrong with her but now she is mended. She tells herself this all the time, so that she can almost start to believe it, almost quell those shouts that say, there is nothing wrong with me, there was never anything wrong with me.

'Better in what way?' Dr Naysmith asks, his pen poised, polished in the sunlight streaming on to his desk. Esme would like nothing more than to reach into its heat, to lay her head on his papers, to feel the burn of it on her face.

'Just better,' she says, her mind racing. 'I . . . I never cry, these days. I'm sleeping well. I'm looking forward to things.' What else, what else? 'My appetite is good. I'm . . . I'm keen to get back to my studies.'

She sees a frown appear on Dr Naysmith's face.

'Or . . . or . . .' she falls over herself '. . . or perhaps I should just like to . . . to help my mother for a while. Around the house.'

'Do you think about men, ever?'

Esme swallows. 'No.'

'And do you still experience these moments of confused hysteria?' he says.

'What do you mean?'

Dr Naysmith peers at something in his notes. 'You insisted clothes that belonged to you weren't yours, a school blazer in particular,' he reads, in a monotone, 'you claimed to see yourself sitting on a rug with your family when you were, in fact, at some distance from them.'

Esme looks at the doctor's lips. They stop moving and

close over his teeth. She looks down at the file before him.
The room seems to have very little air in it: she is having
to breathe down to the bottom of her lungs and she is still
not getting enough. The bones of her head feel tight,
constricted, and the tremor has seized her limbs again. It
is as if this doctor has peeled back her skin and peered
inside her. How can he possibly know about that when the
only person she told was—

'How did you know that?' She hears her voice waver, rise
at the end of the sentence and she tells herself, watch it,
be careful, be very careful. 'How did you hear about those
things?'

'That is not the question. The question, is it not, is
whether you still experience these hallucinations?'

She digs her nails into the flesh of her thighs; she blinks
to clear her head. 'No, Doctor,' she says.

Dr Naysmith writes furiously in his notes and there must
be something in what she says because, at the end of the
appointment, he leans back in his chair, fingertips resting
together in a cage. 'Very good, young lady,' he intones.
'How should you like to go home soon?'

Esme has to suppress a sob. 'Very much.' She manages
to speak these words in a thoughtful voice, to sound not
too eager, too hysterical. 'I would like that very much.'

She runs down the corridor towards the window, which
is illuminated with soft spring light. Before she comes to
the ward door, she cuts her pace to a level, ordinary walk.
Ordinary, ordinary, is the word she incants to herself over

and over again as she enters the ward, as she walks to her bed and sits herself down on it, like a good girl.

—a terrible thing to want—

—sewed the sequins on the evening bag for her. She couldn't do it. In truth, she didn't try very hard. After only two she had stabbed herself in the finger and tangled her thread and dropped the box of sequins. She flung the whole thing aside in a rage, saying, how does anyone stand the tedium of it? I took it up because it had to be done and I sat by the fire while she wandered from the window to the table to the piano to the window again, still ranting about tedium and boredom and how was she to stand it. I said, you're dripping blood on the carpet, so she put her finger in her mouth and sucked it. It took me all evening to sew the sequins and I said she could tell Mother that she'd done it but Mother took one look at it and—

—dropped the flowers on the way up the aisle. I don't know why. I wasn't nervous; I felt peculiarly clear-headed and I was cold in my thin dress, Mother's dress. But everyone gasped when I did this and the girl who was bridesmaid darted round me and picked them up and I heard someone muttering that it was bad luck and I wanted to say, I don't believe in that, I am not superstitious, I am getting married, I am getting married and—

—a terrible thing to want a—

—remember very clearly the first time I saw her. The

ayah, I forget her name, came in and put her hand on my neck and said, you have a little sister. We walked hand in hand round the courtyard and into the bedroom and Mother was lying on her side and Father said, ssh, she's sleeping, and he lifted me so I could see into the crib. The baby was awake and involved in some tussle with her coverlet, and her skin had a pale, waterlogged look to it, as if she belonged to some other element. She had eyes dark as coffee beans and she was watching something just past our heads. What do you think, Father said, and I said, she is the most beautiful thing I have ever seen, and she was, she was—

—a nightgown in rosy silk and I imagined him saying, you are the most beautiful thing I've ever seen. And when he came out of the bathroom and I lay there on the bed, ready in my gown of rose-petal silk, I wasn't nervous. I just wanted it over, so that we could begin, so that my new life could start and I could leave all that behind me. In the train, I had practised writing my new name, Mrs Duncan Lockhart, Mrs K.E. Lockhart, Mrs D.A. Lockhart. I showed him, just for a bit of fun. And he said that he didn't particularly like my name. Kitty, he said, was a name for a pet, a cat perhaps, didn't I think that Kathleen was a more sensible option now that I was—

—a terrible thing, a terrible—

—and so I lay there and it seemed like a dreadfully long time. I couldn't hear anything, no water running, no moving about. Nothing. I had an urge to go up to the bathroom door and press my ear to it, just to be sure he was still in there, and a dreadful thought crossed my mind: what if he had escaped through the window and into the night? But then the door opened and yellow light spread into the bedroom, before he turned it off, and I saw his pyjamaed figure moving through the room, felt the bed sag as he sat down. He cleared his throat. You must be very tired, he said. His back to me. I said, no, not really. I tried to add, darling, but it didn't quite come out. And then a really dreadful thing happened. I found I was thinking about Jamie, about the way his smile lifted his face, the way his hair grew in a peak on his forehead and I turned my head away and I think he saw, because he was lying down by this time. I turned it back and I wanted to say, I wasn't turning away from you, but I couldn't because he leant over and he kissed me on the cheek. He had one hand on my arm and he kissed me on the cheek and he hovered there for a moment and I thought, now, it will happen now, and I was holding my breath and then he said, good night. And I couldn't understand what—

—and I stood there in Mother's room with the letters in my hand and I saw my name on the front and I saw the writing and I saw that they had never been opened so I put my finger under the flap of one and the glue gave easily and I unfolded the sheet and all I saw was, please, please, come soon, and when I saw this I—

—realise I am speaking aloud. Terrible thing, I am saying, to want a child and not be able to have one. A nurse is standing by the table, peering at something on the wall, and she gives me a funny look. She is young. What does she know? What do you know, I say, and—

Iris stands on the threshold of her living room. Alex is slumped in one corner of the sofa, arm outstretched, aiming the remote control. The television startles into life and a man is frowning at them from a studio, pointing at the concentric circles of a storm approaching another part of the country.

She comes to sit next to him, curling her legs underneath her, resting her temple against his shoulder and they look together at the weather map.

Alex scratches his arm, shifts in his seat. 'So I told Fran I'd probably stay.'

'Stay?'

'The night.'

'Oh.' Iris is surprised, but struggles to pretend that she isn't. 'OK. If you like.'

'No.' He shakes his head. 'If you like.'

'What?'

'I'll stay the night if you want me to.'

She straightens up. 'Alex, what are you on about? You know you're more than welcome to stay but—'

He interrupts in the calm, reasoned voice that never fails to enrage her. 'Can you not tell when someone is trying to do you a favour? I thought I'd stay the night in case you were worried. You know. About being alone with Esme.'

'Don't be ridiculous,' she scoffs. 'She is perfectly—'

Alex catches her face between both hands and pulls it close to his. She is so taken aback that for a moment she cannot move. Then she starts to writhe crossly in his grip. He doesn't let go. 'Iris, listen to me,' he says, at their new, close range, 'I am offering to stay to help you out. I don't know if you know this but you're supposed to say "yes" and "thank you" in these situations. Would you like me to stay the night?' He forces her head into a nodding movement. 'Good. That's settled, then. Say "Thank you, Alex," please.'

'Thank you, Alex, please.'

'You're very welcome.' He is still holding her face between his palms. They regard each other for a moment. Alex clears his throat. 'I mean on the sofa,' he says quickly.

'What?'

'I'd sleep on the sofa.'

Iris pulls away. She smooths her hair. 'Of course,' she says.

She turns her attention back to the television screen. It is showing images of a half-collapsed building, a river flooding its banks, a flattened car, thrashing trees.

'Do you remember,' Alex says suddenly, 'when it was that we last slept under the same roof?'

She shakes her head, still looking at the storm pictures.

'Eleven years ago. The night before my wedding.'

Iris doesn't move. She focuses on the frayed edge of his sleeve, the spot of what looks like ink there, the way the lock and weft of the fabric is beginning to unravel.

'Except you were on the sofa that night. Not me.'

Iris remembers the low buzz of a defective light in the corridor outside his tiny apartment in Manhattan's Lower East Side, long hours of jet-lagged wakefulness, an iron bar that seemed to run the length of the sofa just beneath the upholstery. She remembers the boom and wail of the city rising up to the open window. And she remembers Alex appearing next to her in the middle of the night. No, she had said, no. Absolutely not. And she had struggled away. Why, he had said, what's the matter? She hadn't seen him for almost nine months – the longest they had ever been apart. Iris had been in Moscow, as part of her degree course, struggling to teach sullen Russian youths the subtleties of the English pluperfect.

You're getting married, Alex, she had shouted, tomorrow. Remember? And he had said, I don't care, I don't want to marry her. Then don't, Iris replied. I have to, he said, it's all arranged. It can be unarranged, she said, if you want. But he had shouted then: why did you go to Russia, why did you go, how could you leave like that? I had to, she shouted back, I had to go, you didn't have to come to New York, you don't have to stay here, you don't have to marry Fran. I do, he said, I do.

Iris uncurls herself, straightens her legs, places her feet on the floor. She says nothing.

'So, what are you going to do about this Lucas person, then?' Alex asks, fiddling with the remote control.

Iris allows there to be a slight pause before she says: 'Luke.'

'Luke, Lucas,' he waves a hand, 'whatever. What are you going to do?'

'About what?'

Alex sighs. 'Don't be obtuse. Just try it. For once. See how it feels.'

'Nothing,' she says, looking fixedly at the television. She doesn't want to talk about this any more than she wants to talk about the night before Alex's wedding, but she is relieved that at least they seem to be back in the present. 'I don't know what you mean. I'm not going to do anything.'

'What – you're just going to continue as this guy's mistress? Jesus, Iris,' Alex flings the remote to the arm of the sofa, 'do you never feel you're selling yourself short?'

She snaps upright, stung. 'I'm not selling myself in any way at all. And I'm not his mistress. What a hideous word. If you think—'

'Iris, I'm not having a go at you. I just wonder if . . .' He trails off.

'What? You wonder what?'

'I don't know.' Alex shrugs. 'I mean, is he . . . I don't know.' He fiddles with a loose thread in a cushion. 'Is he who you want?'

Iris sighs. She flings herself backwards so that she is lying flat against the cushions. She squeezes her eyes shut, pressing her fingers to them, and when she opens them the room leaps with violent colour. 'He says he's going to leave her.' She addresses the lampshade above her.

'Really?' He is looking at her, she can tell, but she doesn't meet his eye. 'Hmm,' he mumbles, and picks up the remote again. 'I bet he won't. But what would you do if he did?'

From her reclined position, Iris sees Esme enter the room and drift towards them. She has the ability to make herself almost invisible. Iris doesn't know how she does it. She watches her and sees that Esme doesn't look their way, doesn't acknowledge their presence in the room, as if they are invisible to her.

'What?' Iris says, watching Esme. 'Oh, I'd hate it. I'd be horrified. You know that.'

Esme has been distracted from her invisibility thing by something. She stops in her tracks, then approaches a desk Iris keeps pushed up against the wall. Is it the desk she's interested in? No. It's the pinboard above it, where Iris has stuck a patchwork of postcards and photographs. She sees Esme leaning in to look at them. Iris glances back to the television, to the reports of high winds and rain.

Then she turns. Esme has said something, in a peculiar, high voice.

'What was that?' Iris says.

Esme gestures at something on the pinboard. 'There's me,' she says.

'You?'

'Mmm.' She points at the pinboard. 'A picture of me.'

Iris scrambles from the sofa. She is more than keen to leave it and the conversation with Alex. She crosses the room and comes to stand next to Esme. 'Are you sure?' she says. She is sceptical. It's not possible that she has had a photo of Esme on her wall for all these years and not realised it.

Esme is indicating a brown photograph with curling edges that Iris had found among her grandmother's papers. She'd liked it and kept it, pinning it up with the other pictures. Two girls and a woman stand beside a big white car. The woman is wearing a white dress and a hat pulled down over her eyes. A fox hangs about her shoulders, tail snapped in mouth. The elder girl is standing with her head touching the woman's arm. She has a ribbon in her hair, ankle socks, her feet splayed, and her hand rests in that of the younger girl, whose gaze is fixed on something just beyond the lens. Her outline is slightly blurred – she must have moved as the shutter fell. To Iris, it gives her a ghostly appearance, as if she might not have been there at all. Her dress matches that of the other girl but her hair ribbon has come loose and one end hangs down to touch her shoulder. In her free hand is a small, angular object that could be a baby's rattle or a kind of catapult.

'It was in our driveway in India,' Esme is saying. 'We were off on a picnic. Kitty got sunstroke.'

'I can't believe that's you,' Iris says, staring at an image she knows by heart but suddenly cannot recognise. 'I can't believe you're there. Right there. You've been here in front of me all these years and I never knew about you. I've had this photo up by my desk for so long and I've never thought about who the younger girl was. It's stupid. Incredibly stupid of me. I mean, you're wearing matching clothes.' Iris frowns.

'I should have noticed that. I should have wondered about it. It's so obvious that you're sisters.'

'Do you think?' Esme says, turning to her.

'Well, you don't look alike. But I can't believe I never saw it. I can't believe I never asked her who you were. I only found it after she'd become so bad we had to move her out of here.'

Esme is still looking at her. 'How ill is she?' she asks.

Iris bites at a snag in her nail and pulls a face. 'It's hard to quantify. Physically, they say she's in good shape. But mentally it's all a bit of a mystery. Some things she remembers quite clearly and others are just gone. Generally, she's stalled at about thirty years ago. She never recognises me. She's got no idea who I am. In her mind, her granddaughter Iris is a little girl in a pretty frock.'

'But she remembers things from before? From before thirty years ago?'

'Yes and no. She has good days and bad days. It depends when you catch her and what you say.' Iris wonders whether or not to bring this up, but before she has even thought it through, she finds herself saying, 'I asked her about you, you know. I went to see her specially. At first she said nothing, and then she said . . . she said a very strange thing.'

Esme looks at her for so long that Iris wonders if she heard her.

'Kitty,' Iris clarifies. 'I went to see Kitty about you.'

'Yes.' Esme inclines her head. 'I understand.'

'Would you like to know what she said? Or not? I don't have to tell you, I mean, it's up to—'

'I would like to know.'

'She said, "Esme wouldn't let go of the baby."'

Esme turns away, instantly, as if on a pivot. Her hand passes through the air above Iris's desk, past the papers, the envelopes, the pens, the unanswered mail. It comes to a stop near the pinboard. 'This is your mother?' Esme asks, pointing at a snapshot of Iris, the dog and her mother on a beach.

It takes Iris a moment to respond. She is still thinking about the baby, whose baby it might have been, she is still hurtling along a detective track and it takes her a few seconds to slam on the brakes. 'Yes,' she says, attempting to focus on the photo. So you're playing the avoidance game, she wants to say. She touches the next photo along, giving Esme a quick glance. 'That's my cousin, my cousin's baby. There's Alex and my mum again, on top of the Empire State Building. Those are friends of mine. We were on holiday in Thailand. That's my goddaughter. She's dressed as an angel for a nativity play. That's me and Alex when we were children – that was taken in the garden here. This one was at my friend's wedding a couple of months ago.'

Esme looks at each one carefully, attentively, as if she will be examined on them later. 'What a lot of people you have in your life,' she murmurs. 'And your father?' she says, straightening up, fixing Iris with that gimlet gaze of hers.

'My father?'

Maggie O'Farrell

'Do you have a photograph of him?'

'Yes.' Iris points. 'That's him there.'

Esme bends to look. She eases out the drawing-pin and holds the photograph close to her face.

'It was taken just before he died,' Iris says.

—and so I hid from Mother and Duncan and I took a taxi cab. I told them I was going into town but really I went in the opposite direction. As we drove there I kept thinking about how it would be and I pictured a pretty sort of room and her in a nightgown, sitting in a chair with a rug over her knees, looking out over a garden, perhaps. And I pictured her face lighting up when she saw me and how I might help a little, in small ways, straightening the rug for her, perhaps reading a line or two from a book, if she felt up to it. I pictured her taking my hand and squeezing it in gratitude. I was amazed when the driver told me we had arrived. It was so close! Not ten minutes from where we lived. And all that time I had imagined her far away, out of the city. It couldn't have been more than a mile or so, two at most. As I walked up the drive I looked around for other patients but there were none. A nurse met me at the door and she showed me, not to where she was, but to an office where a doctor was fiddling with a fountain pen and he said, it's a pleasure to meet you, Miss— and I said, Mrs. Mrs Lockhart. And he apologised and nodded and he wanted to know. He wanted to know. He said, I have been trying to make contact with your parents. He said—

—and on the sixth night of my marriage, when he got into bed, I reached out for him through the dark. I took his hand in mine and I held it firm. Duncan, I said, and I was surprised at how authoritative I sounded, is everything all right? I had rehearsed this during the day, during the many days, I had decided what I would say. Is it me? I said. Is it something I'm doing or not doing? Tell me what to do. You must tell me. He extracted his fingers from mine. He patted my hand. My dear, he said, you must be tired. On the nineteenth night, he suddenly rolled on to me in the dark. I was just drifting off to sleep. It gave me a shock and I couldn't breathe but I lay still and I felt him grip my shoulder with one hand, like a man testing a tennis ball, and I felt his feet paddling at mine and I felt his other hand pulling up the hem of my nightgown and then he made a kind of frantic, tugging motion somewhere lower down and he shifted the hand on my shoulder to my breast and all I could think was, my God, and then he stopped. He stopped dead. He scrambled off me, back to his side of the bed. Oh, he said, and his voice was full of horror, oh, I thought . . . and I said, what, you thought what? But he never—

—doctor called me Mrs Lockhart and he said, what provisions have your family made for when she comes home? For her and the baby?

*

Sister Stewart appears at Esme's bedside early one morning. 'Get yourself up and get your things together.'

Esme rips back the bedsheets. 'I'm going home,' she says. 'I'm going home. Aren't I?'

Sister Stewart pushes her face up close. 'I'm not saying yes and I'm not saying no. Now, come on. Be quick about it.'

Esme pulls her dress over her head and bundles her possessions into its pockets. 'I'm going home,' she calls to Maudie, as she trips down the ward behind Sister Stewart.

'Good for you, hen,' Maudie replies. 'Come back and see us.'

Sister Stewart walks down two flights of stairs, along a long corridor, past a row of windows, and Esme sees snatches of sky, of trees, of people walking along the road. She's coming out. There is the world waiting for her. It is all she can do to stop herself pushing past Sister Stewart and breaking into a run. She wonders who will have come to collect her. Kitty? Or just her parents? Surely Kitty will have come, after all this time. She'll be waiting in the foyer with the black and white tiles, sitting on a chair perhaps, her bag balanced on her lap, as it always is, her gloves on just so, and as Esme comes down the stairs she will turn her head, she will turn her head and smile.

Esme is about to take the flight of stairs leading to the ground floor and Kitty when she realises Sister Stewart is holding open a door for her. Esme steps through. Then Sister Stewart is speaking to another nurse, saying here's

Euphemia for you, and the nurse is saying, come on, this way, here's your bed.

Esme stares at the bed. It is steel, with a coarse cotton cover and has a blanket folded at its end. It is in an empty room with one window, so high up she can see nothing but grey cloud through it. She turns. 'But I'm going home,' she says.

'No, you're not,' the nurse replies, and reaches out to take her bundle of clothes.

Esme pulls it away. She can feel that she is about to cry. She is about to cry and she does not think she can stop herself this time. She stamps her foot. 'I am! Dr Naysmith said—'

'You're to stay here until the baby comes.'

Esme sees that Sister Stewart is leaning against the wall, watching her, a peculiar smile on her face. 'What baby?' Esme asks.

Her face is so close to the bed-end that she can see marks on the metal. Scratches or chips in the enamel. She is twisted, contorted, her head pushed back into the mattress, her back arched, and she curls her hands over the marks and watches her fingers turn white. The pain comes up from the core of her and seems to engulf her, storming over her head. Such pain is unimaginable. It will not stop. It has her in a constant, never-weakening grip and she does not think she is going to live. Her time is now. Her time is soon. It is not possible to be in so much pain and not die.

She tightens her fingers round the marks and she hears someone screaming and screaming, and only then does it occur to her that they are teethmarks. Someone in this ward, in this very bed, has been driven to gnaw the bedpost. She hears herself shout, teeth, teeth.

'What's she saying?' one of the nurses asks, but she cannot hear the answer. There are two nurses with her, an older one and a younger one. The younger one is nice. She holds her to the bed, like the older one, but not so firmly and, near the beginning of this, she dabbed a cloth over her face when the older nurse wasn't looking.

They are pressing down on her shoulders, on her shins, saying, lie still now. But she cannot. The pain twists her, it lifts her from the bed, buckles her. The nurses thrust her back to the mattress, again and again. Push, they shout at her, push. Don't push. Push now. Stop pushing. Come on, child.

Esme has lost sensation in her legs and arms. She can hear a high-pitched shriek and a panting, like that of a sick animal, and the nurse saying, that's it, that's it, keep going, and she thinks that she has heard these sounds before somewhere, somehow, a long time ago, and is it possible that she could have overheard her mother in labour – with Hugo, with one of those other babies? She seems to see herself tiptoeing up to a door, her parents' door in the house in India, and hearing this same pant-pant-pant and the high ululating and the cries of encouragement. And the smell. This hot, wet, salted smell is something she has encountered before. She sees herself at the door, pushing it open and, through the crack, glimpsing what looks for a moment like a painting. The dim room and the white of the sheet with the startling scarlet and the woman's head dark with sweat, bent over in supplication, the attendants gathered round, the steam from a basin. Is is possible she saw this? She bends her own head, gives three short pants, and even this appearance of a small, slick, seal-being has the unreality of something that has happened already.

Esme turns on to her side and pulls her knees up to her chest. She is washed ashore, shipwrecked. She finds herself examining her hands, which are crumpled near her face. They look the same. And this strikes her as curious, that they should be so unchanged, that they should look just as they have always done. The nurse is severing through something twisted and rope-like and Esme watches as the tiny blue body becomes rinsed with red and the nurse lands a slap on its bottom and turns it over.

Esme raises herself on an elbow. It takes an immense amount of effort. The baby's eyes are shut tight, the fists held up at the cheeks and its expression is unsure, anxious. Look, the nurse says, a boy, a healthy boy. Esme nods. The nurse swaddles him in a green blanket. And Esme says, 'Can I have him?' The nurse, the young one it is, glances towards the door then back to Esme. 'Well,' she says, still holding the baby. 'Quickly, then.'

She comes over and lays him in Esme's arms and the

weight, the balance of him is oddly familiar. His eyes open and he looks up at her and his gaze is grave, calm, as if he'd been expecting her. She touches his cheek, she touches his forehead, she touches his hand, and it opens and locks tight again round her finger.

The older nurse is back in the room and she is saying something about papers, but Esme does not listen. The nurse reaches down for the baby; she puts her hands about him.

'Could we not just give her five minutes?' The younger nurse's voice is soft, pleading.

'No, we can't,' snaps the older one, and she starts to lift the baby out of Esme's arms.

And Esme realises what is happening. She snatches the baby away from the nurse. No, she says, no. She slides off the bed with him and her knees give way beneath her but she crawls away, over the floor, the baby grasped to her chest. Come on, Euphemia, she hears the nurse say behind her, don't be naughty, give me the baby. Esme says that she won't, she won't, get away from me. The nurse seizes her arm. Now, listen, she begins, but Esme turns and lands a punch right in her eye. You little, the nurse mutters, staggering backwards, and Esme finds her strength, raises herself up on her legs. For a second, she cannot balance, strangely light as she is after all these months. But she pushes herself into a run and she makes it past the bed, past the young nurse who, she sees, is coming for her too, towards the door.

She is there, she is there, she is out, she is through, into the corridor, and she is running towards the staircase and the baby is warm and damp against her shoulder and she thinks that now she might be free, that she will take the baby and go home, that they will not turn her away, and that she could keep on running like this for ever but she hears footsteps behind her and someone catches her round the waist.

Euphemia, they say, stop it, stop it now. The nurse is there again, the old bitch, and she is puce with anger. She lunges at the shoulder where Esme has the baby but Esme jerks away. There is an alarm sounding around them. The younger nurse has her hands on the baby, Esme's baby, and she is pulling at him and he starts to cry. It's a small eh-heh, eh-heh, eh-heh sound, near Esme's ear. It is her baby, and she is holding on to him, they are not going to get him but the other nurse has her now, she has her arm bent up and she is twisting it into Esme's back and here is pain again and Esme thinks she can bear it and they will not take her baby, but the nurse has her arm round Esme's neck and is pressing in and it's hard to draw breath and she is struggling and she feels she feels she feels her grip on the baby slipping. No, she tries to say, no, no, please. The nurse is getting him, she is getting him, he is gone. He is gone.

Esme sees the whorl of hair on the crown of his head as the nurse hurries away with him, one clenched starfish hand, she hears the eh-heh eh-heh noise. People, men, big men, are running towards her with straps and needles and jackets. She is pushed to the floor, face down, a puppet without strings, and she sees that all she has of him is the blanket, the green blanket, which has unwound in her hands, empty, and she struggles, she screams, she lifts her head and she sees the feet of the nurse who has her baby, she sees the shoes and the legs as the nurse walks away but she cannot see him. She tries to lift her head further because she wants to see him, one last time, but someone is pushing her face into the tiles and so she must just listen, beneath the screams and the shouts and the alarm, to the footsteps as they recede down the corridor and, eventually, vanish.

—certainly didn't know. I don't think anyone did. I think we all just expected the man to have the knowledge and to get on with it. I certainly never asked Mother and she never said anything to me. I do remember worrying about it beforehand but then my concerns were different. It never occurred to me that he wouldn't know what—

    —and there were times when I would look at her and wonder what it was about her. Her hair was frizzy, she had freckles because she never would wear a hat in the sun, her hands were uncared-for, her clothes were crumpled, carelessly put on. And of course I would feel guilty then because this was my sister and how could I be thinking these uncharitable thoughts? But, still, I would wonder. Why her? Why her and not me? I was prettier, it was often remarked upon, I was older, closer to his age, in fact. I had skills she would never master. I still think, from time to time, that if he hadn't gone away, it might have been possible for me to—

—I heard. I heard it all. I was in a room off the corridor, waiting. A nurse came in, then another, and they shut the door, bang, behind them. They looked flustered and they were both breathing hard. That wee, one of them said, then, seeing me, stopped. And we all listened to the screams. There was a gap in the top of the door, so it was very clear, the noise. And I said—

—and the specialist told me to remove the clothes from the lower half of my body, and it nearly made me sick but I did. I had to look up at the ceiling while he stretched and pulled and I was near to screaming by the time he straightened up. And he was looking nervous. My dear, he said, you are, ah, you are still intact. Do you understand me? I said yes, but the truth was I didn't. Have you not yet, he said, as he fussed about, washing his hands, his back to me, had relations with your husband? I said yes. I said I had. I said I thought I had. Hadn't I? The doctor looked down at his notes and said, my dear, no. And that night I sat on the edge of the bed and I tried not to cry, I tried really hard, and I repeated to Duncan the phrases that the doctor had used, I—

—time for a biscuit, that woman thinks. I wish she would go away. I wish they would all go away. How one can be lonely while constantly surrounded by people is beyond me. How am I to exist if—

—tried to pick up clues, girls did in those days, but it was all so hazy. You knew it happened in bed, at night, and that it was expected to be painful but, beyond that, it was veiled. I did think about asking my grandmother but—

—no, I do not want a custard-cream biscuit. There is nothing I want less. Will these people never—

—and the screaming stopped so suddenly. And after it there was such a silence. I said, what has happened? And the nurse nearest me said, nothing. They've sedated her. Don't you worry, she said, she'll have a nice sleep and when she wakes up she'll have forgotten all about it. And then I saw the baby. I hadn't noticed him until then. The nurse saw me looking and she brought him over to me and put him in my arms. And I gazed down at him and something overcame me. I was close, then, to changing my mind, to saying, no, I don't want him after all. He smelt of her.

He smelt of her.

I have never got over this.

But then I—

—thought they might be words he would understand. I said them to him: penetration, I said, and a release of fluid. I had learnt them like I had learnt French verbs, a long time before. I thought it would help. I thought it might fix the problem. I had put on my rose nightgown. But he leant over and picked up his pillow and then he walked across the room. I think until he reached the door I didn't actually believe he was going. I thought, perhaps he is just pacing about, perhaps he is going to fetch something. But no. He reached the door, he opened it, he left, he shut it behind him. And something in me shut too. And it was only the next day when I hid from him and my parents and I went to the hospital where I was intercepted by the doctor who said—

—the smell of that biscuit is nauseating. I will pick it up and push it under that cushion and that way I won't be able to smell—

—so I gazed down at the baby because I thought I couldn't do it, I thought I would have to give him back, and then I saw who he looked like. I saw it. I don't think, until that moment, I'd fully realised what had happened, what she had done. She had done that with him. And in me rose an anger. How had she known and not me? She was younger than me, she wasn't as pretty as me, she certainly wasn't as accomplished as me, she wasn't even married and yet she had managed to—

—went there because, in truth, I didn't know where else to go. Mother wouldn't have helped and I couldn't have told her, we just didn't have that kind of conversation, the visit to the specialist doctor hadn't helped, in fact it had made it worse. And I did want a baby so badly. It was like an ache in my head, a stone in my shoe. It is a terrible thing to want something you cannot have. It takes you over. I couldn't think straight because of it. There was no one else, I realised, whom I could possibly tell. And I missed her. I missed her. It had been months since she had gone away, so I took a taxi-cab. I was excited, on the way, so excited. I couldn't think why I hadn't done this before. I kept thinking about the look on her face when I walked in.

But when the doctor intercepted me before I got to her and when he said what he said, about her, about a baby, I just—

—never came back to our room. He slept down the corridor, and when Mother died and I inherited the house we moved there and he took the room that had been my grandmother's, while I had the one I had shared with—

And she holds the photograph. She holds it in her hands. She looks at it and she knows. She thinks about those numbers again, the twos and the eights, which together make eighty-two and also twenty-eight. And she thinks about what happened to her once on the twenty-eighth day of a month in late summer. Or, rather, she doesn't think about it. She never needs to. It is running in her mind, always and for ever. She has it, all of the time, she hears it. She is it.

She knows who this man is. She knows who he was. She sees it all now. She glances round the room that used to hold their summer clothes all winter long in cedar chests – lightly folded dresses of cotton and muslin that they hardly ever, in the Edinburgh climate, wore. On bright days in August, they might have shaken them out, aired them, buttoned them on. She doesn't remember how often this happened. But instead of the tall chest with many shallow drawers that her mother found so useful for her print blouses and light shawls there is a television. It casts a guttering, bluish pall over the room.

She looks again at the photograph of the man. He is holding a child on his shoulders. They are outside. Tree branches reach down into the frame from above. He is half tilting his face up to say something to the child. She has her fingers gripped in his hair; his are curled round her ankles, holding her fast, as if he is afraid she might float up into the clouds if he were to let go.

Esme examines the man's face and she sees, in its planes and angles, the set of the head, everything she ever wanted to know. She sees this, she understands this: he was mine. She seems to hold out her arms for this knowledge and she takes it. She puts it on, like an old overcoat. He was mine.

She turns to the girl standing next to her and this girl is so like Esme's mother, so very like, that it could be her − but her in strange, layered clothes and with her hair cropped and cut in an asymmetric slant across the forehead, so unlike how her mother's would ever have been, it makes her almost laugh to think it. And she sees that the girl is hers, too. What a thought. What a thing. She wants to take the girl's hand, to touch that flesh which is her flesh. She wants to hold on to her, fast, in case she might float off and up into the clouds, like a kite or a balloon. But she doesn't. Instead she takes two steps to a chair and sits down, the photograph on her knee.

There is a moment, under sedation, before full unconsciousness swallows you, when your real surroundings leave an impression on that floating, imagistic delirium that holds you under. For a short period you inhabit two worlds, float between them. Esme wonders for a moment if the doctors know this.

So, anyway, they hoisted her up from the floor of the corridor and she was inert, an outsized rag doll. Already, thousands of ants were boiling up out of the ceiling above her, and out of the corner of her eye, she could see a grey dog running along the wall of the corridor, muzzle to the ground.

Two men were carrying her between them, she could be fairly sure of this. An arm and a leg each, her head lolling back on her neck, all the blood rushing cold there, what was left of her hair almost touching the ground. She knew where she was going. She'd been at Cauldstone long enough. The grey dog seemed to be following her, coming with her, but the next moment it had slunk across the corridor and leapt from a window. Could it be open, that window? Was it possible? Probably not. But she did seem to feel a breeze skimming across her skin, a warm breeze, flowing from somewhere, and she saw a person stepping out of a door. But this couldn't be real either because this person was her sister and she appeared upside-down, walking on the ceiling. And she was wearing Esme's jacket. Or a jacket that had been Esme's. One in fine red wool that her sister had always admired. She had her back to Esme and she was walking away. Esme watched with longing. Her sister. Imagine that. Here. She thought of trying to speak, trying to call her name, but the lips don't obey, the tongue won't work and, anyway, she couldn't be real. She never came. She would fly out of the window in a moment, like the grey dog, like all the ants, who were growing wings and crowding into her face with small, hooking feet.

—seemed to fit. That is all. It seemed too good to be true. I did want a baby so much, so very much. It was as if an angel had descended from heaven and said, this could be yours. So I went to Father because nothing could be done without him, of course. I asked to speak to him in his study and he sat behind his desk, staring down at his blotting pad as I spoke. And I finished speaking and he did not reply. I waited, standing there in my good clothes because for some reason I had thought it fit to dress properly to make this request, as if that would help my case. I saw no other way, no other possible end to my torment, you see. I think I said this to him and my voice trembled. And he looked up sharply because he hated nothing more than women crying. He said so often enough. And he sighed. As you see fit, my dear, he said, and he gestured me out of the room. It was astonishing to me, that moment, as I stepped into the hall and I saw that it could happen, that it could be. But I should say quite clearly that I never meant to—

—so remarkably easy. I said to people, I am going away for a few months, south. Yes, I'm going for the air. The doctors say the warmth is best in my condition. Yes, a baby. Yes, it's marvellous. No, Duncan is not coming with me. The office, you know. All so remarkably easy. The only problem with lying is that you have to remember what you've told whom. And this was easy because I told everyone the same thing. It was perfect. Gloriously, unutterably perfect. No one would be any the wiser. I said to Duncan: I'm having a baby, I'm going away. I didn't even look at him to see his reaction. I sometimes think that Mother worked it out. But I can't be sure. Perhaps Father said something although he maintained it was all for the best if she never knew. If she did realise, she never—

—Jamie would come back to Edinburgh once in a while with his French wife and then a small Englishwoman and then, this was in much later years, a silly girl half his age. He held the baby once. He arrived unannounced and I was in the parlour with Robert on a rug on the floor. He was just crawling, I remember. And in he came, alone for once, and Duncan was out and there was the baby on the rug, between us, and he said, aha, the son and heir, and I could not speak. He bent and swept up the baby and held him high above his head and I could not speak and he said, a bonny lad, very bonny, and the baby looked at him. He looked at him very hard, the way babies do, then his lower lip went straight and square and he opened his mouth and howled. He howled and howled. He wriggled and fought and I had to take him back. I had to take him upstairs, away, away, and I was glad. I held him to me, as I climbed the stairs, and I whispered in his ear: I whispered the truth. The first time I'd ever said it. The only time. I said—

—times when it wasn't so easy. Who was it who couldn't

keep a secret and had to whisper it to the river? I don't recall. There were days when it was very hard. If there had been just one other person with whom I could talk it over, could vent myself, it would have been better. I did go back, once, I felt it only right. And they took me down to this terrible place like a dungeon and instructed me to peep through this small hole in a door with iron locks. And in this *camera obscura* I saw a creature. A being. All wrapped up like a mummy but with a face that was bare and split and bleeding. It was creeping, creeping, its shoulder pressed into the softened wall, mumbling to itself. And I said, no, that's not her, and they said, yes, it is. I looked again and I saw that perhaps it was and I—

—and so I said to the doctor, yes, adoption, that will be perfect. I will take it myself. And he said, admirable, Mrs Lockhart. And he said, we will keep Euphemia with us for a while afterwards, to see how she fares, and after that perhaps . . . And I said yes. As simple as that. But I never meant for her to—

Iris lurches into consciousness and lies for a moment, stunned, staring at the ceiling. Something has woken her. A noise, an unfamiliar movement in the house? It's still early, before dawn, the light grey and watery behind the blinds, much of the room in shadow.

She twists on to her side, trying to find a comfortable, uncrushed part of the pillow, pulling the duvet up round her neck. She thinks about Esme, next door in her single bed, and Alex on the sofa. She is just reflecting that her flat is filling up by the day when it suddenly comes back to her what woke her.

It was not so much a dream as a revisitation. Iris had been walking through the lower floors, through the house as it had been in her grandmother's day. Out of the heavy oak door of the parlour, across the hall, past the front door with its patterns of coloured glass, where daylight was pulled and stretched into red triangles, blue squares, up the stairs, her hem swishing round her bare legs, up to the landing. She was just passing the alcove where—

Iris thrashes crossly on to her other side, pummelling and yanking at the pillow. She should read a book. To help get herself back to sleep. She should go to the loo. Or the kitchen to get a drink. But she doesn't want to go out there. She doesn't want to be wandering around in the middle of the night, just in case—

Something else strikes her, making her almost sit up. In the dream, she had been wearing the same dress, a flimsy tea-dress, that she'd been wearing the time she— Iris flings herself on to her back, she scratches wildly at her hair, she kicks at the duvet, she's hot, she's so hot, why is she so hot, why is this bed so fucking uncomfortable? She squeezes her eyes shut and surprises herself by realising she is on the verge of tears. She does not, she absolutely does not, want to think about this.

The same dress as when her grandmother had caught

them. Iris covers her face with her hands. She has buried this so effectively, stopped herself thinking about this so efficiently for such a long time it's as if it never happened. She has managed to rewrite her own history, almost. The time Kitty caught them.

Iris glances quickly at the wall separating her bedroom from the living room. She wants to spit at it, to hurl something at it, to shriek, how dare you? She has no doubt that him being here has cast some malign influence over her sleeping thoughts.

The time Kitty caught them. Iris had been away; it was the end of her first year at university. Sadie and Alex had picked her up at the station and Sadie told her they were stopping at her grandmother's house for tea. Iris and Alex hadn't seen each other for what felt like ages. And, in the dim, brocade-heavy room her grandmother called the parlour, they had to sit next to each other in front of a tray of tiny sandwiches, scones and butter, tea in china cups. Her grandmother conversed about her neighbours, the changes in Edinburgh's one-way system, enquired about Iris's course, and remarked that she was looking rather unkempt.

Iris tried to listen. She tried to eat more than a mouthful of the scone but she was coiled tight as a spring. Alex, next to her on the sofa, was apparently listening intently to everything Kitty said, yet all the time his hand brushed against her thigh, his knuckles grazed the thin fabric of her dress, his sleeve touched her bare arm, his foot knocked hers. Iris had to leave the room. She had to climb the stairs to calm herself, to take some deep breaths in the solitude of the bathroom. But when she came out, turning off the light behind her, she walked back across the landing and, just as she got to the top of the stairs, someone reached out for her, caught a handful of her dress and drew her into the alcove with the tall clock. She and Alex grappled with each other, roughly, quickly, their arms sliding and twining round each other, trying to find a hold that satisfied, that felt close enough. His breathing was hard in her ear and she bit down into the smooth muscle of his shoulder and one of them said, we can't, we have to get back. It was her, Iris thinks. Alex let out a small, desperate groan and he pushed her against the wall, his hands yanking at her dress and there was the ripping sound of seams coming apart, and as Iris heard this she heard something else. Feet coming up the stairs, getting closer and closer. She shoved Alex away just as her grandmother stepped on to the landing. She saw them, she looked at them both, she put one hand to her mouth, then she shut her eyes. For a moment, none of them moved. Then Kitty opened her eyes and her hands began to twist and twist in front of her. Alex cleared his throat, as if he was about to speak, but he said nothing. And Kitty looked at Iris. She looked at her hard and for a long time. It was so disconcerting, so penetrating a look that Iris had had to bite her lip so as not to cry out, so as not to say, please, Grandma, please, don't tell on us.

Kitty had turned. She had gone back down the stairs, taking particular care with each step. Iris and Alex heard her heels tap-tap across the hall, then the parlour door open and shut, and they stood in the half-light of the landing, waiting for the next sound to come, the gasp, the shriek, for Sadie to come pounding up the stairs. They waited a long time, standing apart, not looking at one another. But nothing happened. They waited in the long days that followed, for a phone call, for a visit, for Sadie to say, I need to talk to you both. But, again, nothing. Without telling anyone, Iris switched her degree to include Russian, a decision that meant an imminent departure to Moscow for a year. While she was there, she received news that Alex had gone to work in New York and become engaged to a girl called Fran. One way or another, Iris never touched Alex again.

Iris stares at the crazy paving of cracks in the ceiling above her, her teeth set. She snatches at the duvet, yanks it up, then thrusts it away again. She glares at the separating wall. You shit, she wants to shriek, get out of my house. She'll never get to sleep again now.

But she must have done. Because what feels like a few seconds later, something that must be another dream – a panicked, stop-motion sequence about losing the dog in a crowded station – dissolves abruptly around her. Iris rolls into her pillow, moaning, trying to find her way back. Then, beyond the horizon of the duvet, she sees the hem of a cardigan, three buttons.

Esme is standing beside the bed, arms folded, looking down at her. The room is filled with a vivid, yellow light.

Iris raises her head, pushes her hair out of her eyes. For a moment, she cannot speak. She glances over at the dressing-table and is relieved to see that its surface is empty. She replaced the knives last night.

'Esme,' she croaks, 'are you—'

But Esme interrupts her. 'Can we visit Kitty today?'

'Um.' Iris struggles to sit up. What time is it, anyway? Is she wearing anything? She looks down. Her top half, at least, is dressed – in something green. At this precise moment, Iris has no idea exactly what. 'Sure,' she says. She gropes under the pillow for her watch. 'If . . . if that's what you want.'

Esme nods, turns and leaves the room. Iris falls back to her pillows and pulls the duvet up to her neck. She closes her eyes and the bright morning sun glows red behind her eyelids. It's far too early to be awake on a Sunday morning.

When she gets up, she finds Alex in the kitchen with Esme. They are both leaning over a map of the United States and Alex is talking about a road trip he and Iris took fifteen years ago.

'You OK?' he says, without looking up, as Iris passes him on the way to the sink.

She makes a slight noise of assent as she turns on the gas under the kettle. She leans against the hob. Alex is pointing out the location of a national park famous for its cacti.

'You're up early,' she remarks.

'Couldn't sleep. Your sofa's horribly uncomfortable, you

know.' Alex stretches, his T-shirt riding up his body, displaying his navel, the line of hair disappearing into the low-slung waistband of his jeans. Iris looks away, looks at Esme, wondering if it might be a bit much for her. But Esme is still bent over the map.

'It feels weirdly like jet-lag,' Alex continues. 'But obviously it can't be. I don't know what it is. Lag of some sort. Life-lag, maybe. Sofa-lag.'

Iris frowns. It's too early for conversations like this.

There is still an hour or so to kill before visiting time starts at Kitty's home, so Iris takes Alex and Esme up Blackford Hill. Iris turns her head as she walks, taking in the glassy grey of the sea in the distance, the city spread between the hill and the coast, the straggling bushes of gorse, Esme, walking with her fingers splayed out, dress fluttering in the breeze like a curtain at a window, Alex, some distance off, throwing sticks for the dog, a red kite jerking in the breeze, the car park, a few cars, a woman pushing a pram, a man getting out of his car and Iris is thinking that he is attractive, good-looking, before she is thinking that there is something familiar about him, his hair, the way he is rubbing the back of his neck, the way he is taking that woman's hand.

Iris stops in her tracks. Then she turns. She could run. He won't see her, they won't see her, maybe she can just sneak past to her car and they need never meet. But he is turning to put his arm round his wife and, as he does so, his gaze passes over Iris. Iris waits, immobile, turned to a pillar of salt. The instant he sees her, he removes his arm from his wife's shoulders. Then he is hesitating, wondering what to do, whether just to get into his car, with his wife, shut the doors and drive away.

But the wife has seen her. It is too late. Iris watches as the wife says something to him, something questioning. They leave the car, with its doors open, ready for them, and come towards her. He has no choice, she can see that, but she is seized with an impulse to dart away, to escape. If she ran now, this wouldn't have to happen. But Esme is next to her, Alex is over there. How could she leave them?

'Iris,' Luke says.

Iris does a bad imitation of someone recognising someone else. 'Oh, hello.'

Luke and his wife come to a stop before them. He may have taken his arm from round her but the wife has kept hold of his hand. Sensible woman, Iris thinks. There is a pause. She looks at Luke for guidance. How is he going to play this? Which way will he jump? But he is focusing on someone else, and she realises that Alex has materialised at her elbow, the dog's stick still in his hands.

'Hi, Luke,' he says, flinging the stick high into the air, making the dog race off at an angle. 'Haven't seen you for a while. How are you doing?'

Iris sees Luke give a kind of flinch. 'Alexander,' Luke says, with a cough.

'Alex,' Alex corrects.

Luke manages a nod. 'It's good to see you.'

Alex does a curious sideways movement of his head, which somehow manages to convey the message, I remember you, and also, I don't like you. 'Likewise,' he says.

Luke raises himself up on his toes, then starts nodding. Iris finds that she is nodding too. They nod at each other for a moment. He cannot meet her eye and his face is heated, and Iris has never seen him flush before. She finds she cannot look at the wife. She tries, she tries to pull her gaze in that direction, but every time she gets near an odd thing happens and her eyes veer away, as if the wife exudes some negative forcefield too strong for her. The silence is growing, clouding the air between them all, and Iris is raking about for things to say, for excuses, for reasons they have to go when, to her horror, she realises that Alex is speaking: 'So,' he is saying, in a dangerously chatty tone, 'this must be your wife, Luke. Aren't you going to introduce us?'

Luke turns to his wife, as if he'd forgotten all about her. 'Gina,' he says, to the ground between them, 'this is . . . Iris. She . . . We, ah, we . . .' he falters. There is a gaping pause and Iris is curious about what he will say next. What could it possibly be? We fuck whenever we get the chance? We met at a wedding while you were in bed with flu? She wouldn't give me her number so I found out where she worked and went there every day until she agreed to go out with me? She's the one I'm planning to leave you for? 'She . . . she has a shop,' he finishes, and there is a smothered, choked sound from Alex and Iris knows that he is trying not to laugh and she makes a mental note to make him sorry later, sorrier than he's ever been.

But Gina is smiling and reaching out, and her face is empty of guile, empty of jealousy. As she takes her hand, Iris thinks: I could ruin your life. 'Nice to meet you,' she mutters, and she cannot look at this person, she cannot take in an image of the woman she is betraying, the woman who shares his house, his bed, his life. She would like to but she cannot.

But Iris does look at her, she makes herself look, and she sees that Gina is a small woman with pale hair held back in a band, and that she is holding a pair of binoculars, and as Iris focuses on the binoculars she sees something else. Gina is pregnant. Unmistakably pregnant – her body pushed out beneath a black woollen sweater.

Iris stares for long enough to take this in. She sees the interlocking weave of the sweater's fabric, she sees the silver catch on the binoculars' case, she sees that Luke's wife has had a manicure recently and that her nails are painted in the French style.

Iris has the sensation of sinking, of her pulse knocking at her temples, and she would really like to leave, like to be anywhere else but here, and Gina is saying something to Luke and there is a little interchange between them about how cold it is and whether they will walk to the summit of the hill and, in the middle of all this, Esme suddenly turns to look at Iris. She frowns. Then she takes Iris's wrist.

'We have to leave,' she announces. 'Goodbye.' She pulls

Iris away and steers her down the path, glaring at Luke as they go.

When the car pulls up outside the home, Iris observes that her hands haven't stopped shaking, that her heartbeat is still uneven, still fast. She opens and shuts the glovebox as Alex gets out, as he helps Esme do the same. She pulls down the mirror and has a quick glance at herself, decides she looks deranged, pushes her hair off her face, then opens her door and steps out.

As they walk across the car park and in through the glass doors, she avoids meeting Alex's eye. He lopes along beside them, hands in his pockets. Iris passes her arm through Esme's and walks with her to the front desk, where she signs them in.

'Do you want to come as well,' she addresses the region of Alex's shoulder, 'or wait here? I don't mind, it's up to—'

'I'll come,' he says.

At the door to Kitty's room, Iris says, 'Here we are,' and Esme stops. She looks up to her left, at the point in the corridor where the wall meets the ceiling. It is the movement of someone who has just seen a bird passing overhead or felt a sudden gust of wind. She looks down again. She folds her hands over each other, then lets them dangle back to her sides.

'In here?' she says.

The room is bright, sun glaring through the French

235

windows. Kitty is seated in a chair, her back to the view. She is dressed in a taupe twinset, a tweed skirt, a pair of polished brogues, looking for all the world as if she is about to get to her feet and tackle a good country walk. Iris can tell that the hairdresser has visited recently – her hair is brushed back in silver-blue waves.

'Grandma,' Iris advances into the room, 'it's me, Iris.'

Kitty swivels her head to look at her. 'Only in the evenings,' she replies, 'very rarely during the day.'

Iris is momentarily stalled by this but then rallies herself. 'I'm your granddaughter, Iris, and—'

'Yes, yes,' Kitty snaps, 'but what do you want?'

Iris sits on a footstool near her. She feels suddenly nervous. 'I've brought some people to see you. Well, one person, really. The other one, the man over there, is Alex. I don't know if you remember him but . . .' She takes a deep breath. 'This is Esme.'

Iris turns to look at Esme. She is standing beside the door, very still, her head on one side.

'What have you done to your hair?' Kitty shrieks, making Iris jump. She turns back and sees that Kitty is speaking to her.

'Nothing,' she says, wrong-footed. 'I had it cut . . . Grandma, this is Esme. Your sister, Esme. Do you remember your sister? She's come to visit you.'

Kitty doesn't look up. She looks determinedly at her watchstrap, rolling it between her fingers, and the thought crosses Iris's mind that she sometimes understands more than she lets on. Something in the room flexes and stirs, and Kitty rolls the watchstrap, a chain of gold links, between her fingers. Someone somewhere is playing a piano and a thin voice floats out over the top of the melody.

'Hello, Kit,' Esme says.

Kitty's head jerks round and the words begin to fall out of her mouth, without pause or reflection, as if she's had them ready: '– sit there with your legs like that, over the chair arm? Whatever it was you were reading anyway. And what was I supposed to do? My chances all ruined. You look just the same, just the same. It wasn't me, you know. It wasn't. I didn't take it. Why would I have wanted it? The very idea. Anyway, it was for the best. You have to admit that. Father thought so too, and the doctor. I don't know why you've come, I don't know why you're here, looking at me like that. It was mine, it was mine all along. Ask anyone.' She lets go of the watchstrap. 'I didn't take it,' she says, quite distinctly. 'I didn't.'

'Take what?' Iris says, solicitous, leaning forward.

Across the room, Esme unfolds her hands. She places them on her hips. 'But I know that you did,' she says.

Kitty looks down. She plucks and plucks at the fabric of her skirt, as if she can see something stuck to it. Iris looks from one to the other, then at Alex, who is standing beside Esme. He shrugs and pulls a face.

Esme steps further into the room. She touches the bed, the patchwork coverlet, she looks out of the window, along the sweep of the garden, out at the roofs of the city. Then she moves towards her sister's chair. She looks at Kitty for a moment, then reaches out and touches her hair, as if to smooth it into place. She puts her hand to the silver-blue waves at Kitty's temple and holds it there. It is a strange gesture and lasts for only a moment. Then she removes it and says to the air around her, 'I would like to be left alone with my sister, please.'

Alex and Iris walk down the corridor. They walk quickly. At some point, one of them reaches for the other's hand, Iris couldn't say for certain which of them it was. They hold hands, anyway, fingers laced together, and they walk round each corner and out into the sunshine. They walk as far as the car and then they stop.

'Jesus,' Alex says, and exhales as if he's been holding his breath. 'What was all that about? Do you know?'

Iris tilts her head to look at him. The sun is behind him and he is just a black silhouette, blurred and smudged against the light. She extracts her hand from his and leans against the car, pressing her palms against the heated metal. 'I don't know,' she says, 'but I think . . .'

'You think what?' Alex comes to lean next to her.

She pushes herself away from the car. Her arms hurt as if she hasn't moved them for a long time. She tries to order her thoughts. Kitty and Esme. Esme and Kitty. Chances all ruined. Wouldn't let go of the baby. Mine all along but I know that you did. 'I think I don't know.'

'Eh?'

She doesn't reply. She unlocks the car and gets in,

behind the wheel, and after a moment Alex joins her. They sit together in the car, looking out at a man with a mower, cutting the lawn in even stripes, at an elderly resident of the home making his way down a path. She is thinking about Esme and Kitty but is also conscious of something pressing on her that she needs to say to Alex.

'I didn't know,' she says absently. 'I didn't know about the wife. Being pregnant. I would never have . . .'

Alex is looking across at her, his head tilted back into the seat. He gazes at her for a long moment. 'Ah, love,' he says, 'I know.'

They sit in the car together. Alex reaches over for her hand, her left hand, and Iris lets him take it. It lies there, in the lap of his jeans. He straightens out each of her fingers, one by one, then lets them curl back. 'Do you ever wonder,' he says, in a low voice, 'what it is we're doing?'

Iris looks at him. She is still running and rerunning the words in her head. I didn't take it. But I know that you did. 'Sorry?' she says.

'I said,' he speaks again in a soft tone, so that Iris has to strain forward to hear him, 'do you ever wonder what we're doing? You and me?'

Iris stiffens. She readjusts her position; she touches the steering-wheel. The elderly resident has reached the shade of a tree and is gazing up into the branches at something. A bird, perhaps? Iris gives her hand a small tug but Alex holds it fast.

'It's only ever been you,' he says. 'You know that.'

Iris snatches away her hand, pops the catch on the door and opens it with such force that it swings back on its hinges with a grinding noise. She leaps from the car and stands with her back to it, hands over her ears.

Behind her, she hears the other car door open, his feet on the gravel. She whips round. Alex is leaning on the car roof, and with one hand he is extracting a cigarette from its packet. 'What are you so afraid of, Iris?' He gives her a smile as he presses down on his lighter.

Esme holds the cushion between both hands. Its fabric – a textured damask in a deep burgundy – is packed tight with foam stuffing. It has gold piping at its edges. She turns it over, then turns it back. She takes two steps across her sister's room and she places it back on the sofa. She does this carefully, propping it against its twin, making sure it looks exactly as it did when she found it.

Two women in a room. One seated, one standing.

Esme waits for a moment, looking out of the window. The trees shake their heads at her. The sun appears from behind a cloud and shadows slide out from under everything: the tree, the sundial, the rocks round the fountain, the girl, Iris, who is standing beside her car with the boy. They are arguing again and the girl is angry, gesticulating and whirling one way then the other. Her shadow turns and turns with her.

Esme backs away from the window, keeping the girl and boy in her sights. She keeps her face averted from the other. If she is very careful she will not have to think about this just yet. If she holds her head just so, she can almost imagine that she is alone in the room, that nothing at all has happened. It is a relief that the noise has stopped, that everything is still. Esme is glad of that. One seated, one standing. Her hands feel empty now she has put down the cushion so she presses them together. She sits. She continues to press her hands together, with as much force as she can muster. She stares down at them. The knuckles turn white, the nails pink, the tendons standing out under the skin. She keeps her face averted.

Behind her, by the bed, a red cord hangs from the ceiling. Esme saw it when she entered the room. She knows what it is. She knows that if she pulls it, a bell will ring some-where. In a moment, she will get up. She will cross the room. She will cross the carpet, keeping her face averted so she doesn't have to see anything because she doesn't want to see it again, doesn't want it imprinted on her mind any more than it is, any more than it will be, and she will pull the red cord. She will pull it hard. But for now she will sit here. She will take just a few minutes for this. She wants to watch until the sun goes in again, until the sundial loses its marker, until the garden sinks into softness, into shadow.

*

'I'm not afraid of anything!' Iris shouts. 'I'm certainly not afraid of you, if that's what you mean.'

He takes a long draw on his cigarette and seems to consider this. 'I never suggested you were.' He shrugs. 'I just happen to make it my business to interfere in your life. Especially when your life concerns mine too.'

Iris looks about wildly. She considers making a run for it, she considers leaping into the car and driving off, she contemplates the stones beneath her feet and thinks about hurling a handful at Alex. 'Stop it,' she falters instead, 'just stop it. It was . . . it was all so long ago and we were just children and—'

'No, we weren't.'

'Yes, we were.'

'We weren't. But I'm not going to argue the toss with you about that. We're not children now, are we?' He grins at her as he releases a cloud of smoke. 'The point is that you know it's true. It's only ever been you and you know it's only ever been me.'

Iris stares at him. She cannot see how to respond. Her head feels blank, smooth, optionless. Suddenly, somewhere behind her, there is a flurry of feet on gravel and Iris turns, startled. Two carers in white uniforms are hurrying towards the home. One is holding a pager. Iris scans the front of Kitty's building. There is a quick movement behind one of the windows, which vanishes when she looks.

'The thing is, Iris,' Alex says, behind her, 'I just think—'

'Shush,' she urges, still looking at the building. 'Esme . . .'

'What?'

'Esme,' she repeats, pointing at the home.

'What about her?'

'I have to . . .'

'You have to what?'

'I have to,' she begins again, and suddenly something that has been snagged at the periphery of her mind seems to slide forward, the way a boat might loosen from its moorings and float free. Mine all along. Wouldn't let go. And do you have a picture of your father. Iris puts her hand to her mouth. 'Oh,' she says. 'Oh, God.'

She begins to move, slowly at first, then much faster, towards the building. Alex is close behind, calling her name. But she doesn't stop. When she reaches the door of the home, she wrenches it open and sprints along the corridor, taking the turns so fast that she glances off the wall with her shoulder. She has to get there first, she has to reach Esme first, before anyone else, she has to say to her, she has to say, please. Please tell me you didn't.

But when she reaches Kitty's room, the corridor is filled with people, residents in slippers and gowns and people in uniform spilling out of the door, and faces are turning to look at her, pale as handprints.

'Let me through,' Iris pushes at these faces, at these people, 'please.'

In the room are more people, more limbs and bodies and voices. So many voices, clamouring and calling. Someone is telling everyone to move off, to please return to their rooms immediately. Someone else is shouting into a telephone and Iris cannot make out the words. There is a frantic movement by two people leaning over someone or something in a chair. She glimpses a pair of shoes, a pair of legs. Good-quality brogues and thick woollen tights. She turns away her head, closing her eyes, and when she opens them again she sees Esme. She is sitting by the window, her hands laced over her knees. She is looking straight at Iris.

Iris sits down next to her. She takes one of her hands. She has to prise it from the grasp of the other and it feels very cold. She cannot think what she was going to say. Alex is there with her now, she feels the brief pressure of his hand on her shoulder and she can hear his voice telling someone that, no, they can't have a word and will they please back off. Iris has an urge to reach out and touch him, just for a moment. To feel that familiar density of him, to make sure it is really him, that he is really there. But she cannot let go of Esme.

'The sun didn't go in,' Esme says.

'Sorry?' Iris has to lean forward to hear her.

'The sun. It never went in again. So I pulled it anyway.'

'Right.' Iris clutches Esme's hand in both of hers. 'Esme,' she whispers, 'listen—'

But the people in uniform are upon them, muttering, exclaiming, enveloping them in a great white cloud. Iris cannot see anything but starched white cotton. It presses against her shoulders, her hair, it covers her mouth. They are taking Esme, they are pulling her up from the sofa, they are trying to extract her hand from Iris's. But Iris does not let go. She grips the hand tighter. She will go with it, she will follow it, through the white, through the crowd, out of the room, into the corridor and beyond.

Acknowledgements

My thanks to:

William Sutcliffe, Victoria Hobbs, Mary-Anne Harrington, Ruth Metzstein, Caroline Goldblatt, Catherine Towle, Alma Neradın, Daisy Donovan, Susan O'Farrell, Catherine O'Farrell, Bridget O'Farrell, Fen Bommer and Margaret Bolton Ridyard.

A number of books were invaluable during the writing of this novel, in particular *The Female Malady: Women, Madness and English Culture, 1830–1980'* by Elaine Showalter (Virago, London, 1985) and *Sanity, Madness and the Family* by R.D. Laing (Penguin, London, 1964).